FALLEN DESTINY

"Sfetsos is simply one of the best, and *Fallen Destiny*—thrilling, intense, and filled with suspense—displays an artist at the top of her game."
—Brian Bowyer, author of *Metro Kinetic*

"I've been a fan of Yolanda Sfetsos for years, and whether you're brand-new to her work or you've loved her books for as long as I have, *Fallen Destiny* is an absolute must-read. This cozy dark fantasy takes you on a supernatural adventure with page-turning prose and characters you'll adore. Enjoy the ride."
—Gwendolyn Kiste, Four-time Bram Stoker Award-winning author of *The Haunting of Velkwood* and *Reluctant Immortals*

"*Fallen Destiny* is a wicked urban fantasy that will appeal to fans of Kim Harrison. Sfetsos delves into the mysteries of heaven and hell while wrapping the reader in the warm embrace of found family. Move over Hellboy, there's a new kick ass demon in town, and Destiny won't be denied."
—Angela Sylvaine, Bram Stoker Award nominated author of *Frost Bite*

Fallen Destiny

Yolanda Sfetsos

Fallen Destiny

Edited by: Somer Canon

Formatted by: Stephanie Ellis

Cover illustration by: Alison Flannery

First Edition: November 2025

ISBN (paperback): 978-1-963355-39-0

ISBN (ebook): 978-1-963355-38-3

Library of Congress Control Number:

BRIGIDS GATE PRESS
Overland Park, Kansas
www.brigidsgatepress.com
Printed in the United States of America

*For all the fictional paranormal, occult, supernatural investigators who've
kept me entertained for years, and sparked my own creations.*

"What you seek is seeking you."
—Rumi

CHAPTER ONE

"I need you to find me an angel."

"*Ooookay*, sure. Are you looking for one in particular or will any old angel do?" I'd been hired to find a lot of strange things in my time, but no one ever requested an actual angel. Even *I* wouldn't know where to start looking for a celestial. How did one lose an angel anyway?

Was this a joke? I almost asked if it was Kenan calling. If he managed to get his nose out of his books for longer than a second, he might pull such a stunt.

"It's actually a very particular one," the calm voice said. "But I don't feel comfortable talking about it over the phone."

"What did you say your name was?"

"I didn't."

Of course you didn't. That's why I'm asking.

Usually, at that point, I would tell the caller to contact the Sagar Investigations office and promptly hang up because potential clients were supposed to follow the correct process. If they didn't, it spoke volumes about their character and how many problems we might run into at a later date.

If a prospective client can't follow the rules beforehand, what's going to make them change their careless habits? Zenda had drummed the mantra into me the day I'd graduated from apprentice to full-fledged Private Investigator of the Weird Kind.

Besides, I rarely received direct calls, unless it was from one of my handful of friendly contacts. And while in the middle of a transaction, I wasn't ready to add a new item to my to-do list.

The noise level got louder around me as more people arrived at the convention. I'd attended too many of these get-togethers when meeting clients to remember the fandom. Was it for comic book enthusiasts, horror freaks, sci-fi fanatics, or fantasy fiends? It didn't matter, as long as I blended in.

"Look, if you don't mind, I'd appreciate you calling the office directly," I said.

"Oh, right …" Crackling ate the rest of the caller's answer before cutting off completely.

"Hello? Are you there?" I couldn't hear anything but waited a moment in case the connection returned. "Hello?" I pulled the phone away from my ear and found my home screen.

Oh well, guess they hung up. Which was probably for the best.

I didn't have the patience to mess around with secretive individuals. There were enough smoke and mirrors involved in these cases already. I didn't appreciate being forced to pry information from someone reaching out to *me*. If people were serious about needing help, they'd go through the correct channels.

I checked the time and stuck my mobile in the back pocket of my jeans. People congregated inside the hall leading to the real action in the many open areas, but too many were eyeballing me. Staying on the outskirts, away from the stalls and the lines waiting to meet B-list celebrities, wasn't working.

"Wow, her cosplay outfit is awesome," a girl said to her partner as they strolled past.

He snuck a full-body stare. "Yeah, but what's she supposed to be?"

"Can't you tell?" She rolled her eyes. "You should've worn your glasses. Obviously, she's a sexy hellish minion from that pervy comic book you like so much. Look at her tail and horns. So cool!"

"Oh," he said with a nod. "It's not my eyes. I just didn't recognize her with clothes on."

The girl smacked the guy in the arm and met my gaze.

I winked and she smiled back. She might be wrong about the supposed inspiration for my *costume*, but at least she'd gotten the classification right. That was the reason I didn't mind meeting people at these places. I could let my glamour fade away for a while. Not be restricted underneath the intricate layers of concealment magic my favorite witch concocted.

It was only a matter of time before I could officially mark another case as done, and I couldn't wait to get rid of the enchanted item. The neatly folded pelt felt as soft as suede. The gray color glowed silver under the grimy lights, and holding it flooded my mind with the sounds of the ocean and the smell of the beach. I could taste salt on my lips and as I rubbed my fingertips over the surface, a sea breeze stirred my long hair.

I wanted to leave the convention hall and run out to the shoreline. To wrap myself in this beautiful coat and walk into the water. I could practically feel the waves licking at my ankles and calves, enclosing over my shoulders and eventually my head.

"Hello?" a voice called out to me, but my mind was already lost to the sea.

The solid walls melted away until I stood on the beach with the wind whipping strands of hair into my face and the storm clouds swelling in the sky. Waves foamed over my cloven hooves and the ocean called out to me so loudly I started unfolding the coat.

I wanted the water to engulf me completely.

"Can you hear me?"

A hard yank against the pelt dragged me out of my reverie, back into the stifling hall and the energized murmur of fandom.

The ocean and all its smells and wonders vanished.

My hands were suddenly empty and the realization made my stomach lurch. My tail whipped forward of its own accord, wrapped around the ankles of the asshole who'd taken my treasure, and wrenched him off his feet.

He tripped and ended up on his back.

"What the fuck do you think you're doing?" It only took a few steps to catch up to him so I could press a cloven hoof against the culprit's chest, pushing into his sternum. I leaned closer, inspecting the thief with narrowed eyes. He wasn't anything special, just another average man with messy dark hair and an unshaven face who could easily blend into this growing crowd without detection.

Yet an air of malice emanated from him, made my nose tingle and skin crawl. Recognizing cruel intentions was second nature to me.

"I ... it's ..." He squirmed under the pressure, which wasn't surprising because I always underestimated my own strength.

I yanked the pelt from his greedy hands. Back in my possession, I made sure not to lose my head to its magical pull. I fortified my mind in a way that came naturally and shouldn't fail me, as it had done, only moments ago.

Even the demonic get caught up in whimsy when they're too relaxed.
Or bored.

I decreased the pressure on the man's chest.

He coughed, licked his lips. "Oki sent me to pick it up."

I doubt that very much.

A selkie wouldn't hire me to search for her *missing* skin and then send another person to retrieve it.

I narrowed my eyes until they were slits. "You look very familiar."

"I'm Oki's husband!"

My pulse quickened and I dug my hoof harder against his chest. "You mean her *estranged* husband." Of course! I'd seen the photos she'd shown me. He might be disheveled and had lost the fake smile, but he was definitely the bastard who'd betrayed her.

"No, we're still together." His light eyes widened and spittle spotted his chin. "We're soulmates! We will never be apart." He eyed the selkie skin, giving himself away.

The kind of love this man desired was no love at all. Taking a selkie's coat when they chose to live on land as a human would trap them forever. Hiding it enslaved them to the person who possessed the most intimate part of themselves.

"That's not how she tells it." According to Oki, her husband took her skin for ransom the day she told him she planned to return to the sea. I'd spent over three weeks tracking the pelt down, and when I found it, couldn't believe the bastard hadn't even bothered to hide it. Instead, he'd draped the missing part of Oki over his parents' bed, inside his childhood home.

Turned out, breaking into the old couple's house using the key Oki gave me had been the easy part, because this asshole was harder to shake. He'd either been tapping into her phone somehow, or had followed me.

"We had a simple misunderstanding," he said, shaking his head. "That's all."

"Stealing a vital part of someone isn't a misunderstanding." I knew firsthand how it felt to have essential parts taken from you. Or in my case, fade away.

His eyes hardened and the good-guy/poor-guy act dropped as quickly as a curtain on opening night at the theatre. "That coat belongs to me," he spat. "Just like she does."

"I don't think so. This is hers. *Only* hers."

His face turned red but a horrible smirk quirked his lips. "Not anymore."

"What does that mean?" I unhooked my tail from his ankle and wrapped the end around his neck. "Where is she?"

"Give me the skin ... and I'll tell you."

I squeezed. No amount of glamour could hide what was going on in this very public place, but I didn't care. A woman's life was at stake. "Where. Is. She?"

He laughed but it turned into a coughing fit when I applied pressure. "Answer me!"

He laughed louder.

"Answer me, you asshole."

He didn't, and his horrid laughter made my skin itch. It blinded me with rage. My eyesight narrowed into horizontal view until all I could focus on was the fiery pentagram glowing beneath him.

I couldn't let him walk away and cause Oki further harm when her only sin had been to fall in love with the jerk. No one deserved to have their freedom stripped away in such a callous manner. And I was going to make sure he never harmed her, or anyone else, again.

"What're … you … doing?" His face was tomato-red as he attempted to lift his spine off the floor. "That burns!"

I unwound my tail enough for him to take rapid breaths and get a fake sense of safety, but he wasn't going anywhere. The ground opened up and he tumbled into the fire below, screaming until the hole sealed before my eyes and my vision stabilized.

Even though my glowing pentagram was filled with flames, it led to a dark place.

Several shallow breaths allowed my breathing to get back to normal and the sulfur smell to settle into my lungs, revitalizing me in a way no other smoke ever could. I'd tried cigarettes, but they didn't cut it because of the chemicals. Pot was the closest I could get but the smell stuck to everything.

"Oh my god. How did you do that?" A teenage girl rushed over. "That was amazing!"

I didn't answer, wouldn't have been able to even if I wanted because my senses were out of whack. I just hoped nobody had filmed what happened.

Subconsciously opening a portal to the netherworld came easy to me whenever my anger boiled over, or I wanted to right an injustice, but I paid for the effort later. And if that wasn't enough, I had to find the woman who needed me before it was too late.

Where are you, Oki?

I closed my eyes and focused on the pelt in my hands. I was good at finding things, and even better at locating missing *people* because I possessed the talent of the displaced. *It's true what they say, it takes one to know one.* Or in my case, to find the lost.

As my vision cleared, I managed to take one step followed by another until I felt strong enough to walk without my joints locking up on me. I rushed past the crowd and ignored the disgruntled actions, insults, and compliments. I didn't stop until I was outside and a mouthful of ocean air helped clear my head completely.

I stood at the top of the stairs leading to the beach and the preternatural tug led me to the sand.

On shaky legs, I rushed down the stairs. The leaked sulfur from the pentagram had already infused my internal organs and the fresh air helped clear my mind. So it didn't take long to reach the shoreline and find the bleeding woman lying in a fetal position on the clumpy sand near the rocky outcrop.

She seemed withered and small, with long strands of straight hair tangled in seaweed and stuck to her blotchy skin. The blood blended with the waves, frothing back out to sea from the gut wound her husband had inflicted.

"Oki."

She startled and her eyelids fluttered.

Seagulls and sea eagles circled overhead. I wasn't sure if the birds were trying to protect her or waiting until she took her final breath.

"Oki," I repeated, dropping to the wet sand beside her. I should staunch her bleeding but was it too late?

"You … found …" Her wet fingers reached for the coat I'd forgotten I was carrying.

"Yes, I did." My mind raced back to the conversation I'd had with Kenan when I'd first taken on this case only last week. I'd asked him to tell me everything he knew about selkies because he was my go-to guy for supernatural facts.

The selkie skin can restore them.

I unfolded the hide and threw it over Oki's bleeding body like a blanket. The coat joined with her body, adjusted over her spine and limbs, before fusing with her ribcage. She was no longer a dying person, but a seal with a human face. She hadn't allowed the magic to fully grab her yet.

"Thank you," Oki whispered, taking my hand. Her face was fading fast, and her other hand had already transformed into a flipper, which she pressed against her swollen belly. "We can finally … be free."

"Will you be all right out there?" She might be a supernatural seal but plenty of predators called the sea home. Only yesterday, sharks were spotted off this very coast.

Oki nodded. "The ocean will heal and protect us."

"What about the sharks?"

"They won't … hurt us."

I nodded and squeezed her cold fingers before they also became a flipper. "Go and find peace. He'll never bother you again."

Oki's face was engulfed completely and the black eyes of a seal stared back at me. Her coarse whiskers stood out against her silvery skin. She'd become an animal but retained humanity in her stare.

I gave her a push when the waves swept closer and stayed on my knees until she rolled into the water and swam out to sea on her own.

"Take care, my friend." I waved and Oki shook a flipper before diving into the water and splashing her tail one last time.

I wasn't sure how long I stayed on the wet sand staring out at the ocean and the swell of storm clouds, but I didn't stir until my phone buzzed in my pocket. I dug it out without checking the screen. Between the conniving husband and the injured wife, I was wiped, so I didn't bother to see who was calling. Considering the weird call I'd gotten earlier, maybe I should have.

Too late now. "Hello?"

"Des, it's me. We need you at the office."

My heart skipped a beat. "Hey, Kenan, is there a problem?"

"When isn't there a problem around here?" A brief pause. "Are you busy?"

"Just wrapped up another case."

"The selkie?"

I sighed. "Yeah."

"How did it go?"

I wanted to tell him everything, but decided to condense my answer. "She's back where she belongs."

"That's good," he said. "Please get over here as soon as you can."

"On my way." No point in pushing for more, so I disconnected and stood up. I didn't bother wiping the sand off my knees and instead headed for my beloved car, Lady Bug.

As I spotted her tarnished frame in the parking lot, I couldn't help but smile. She might be noisy but she was a dependable thing of beauty. An old semi-restored 1963 Volkswagen Beetle that used to be black but had matured into a blotchy patina resembling her namesake.

I patted her curvy side panel and said, "Let's see what's waiting for us back at the office."

Chapter Two

"Hey!"

The front door swung open before I had the chance to stick the key in the lock. I was too busy leaning over, wiping away the few grains of sand left on the knees of my black jeans. I'd removed most of the clumpy mess before getting into Lady Bug back at the beach, but a few stubborn bits had decided to stick around. The fabric had dried crinkly and my knees felt like they were encased in sandpaper.

"What happened to your jeans?"

"I was kneeling in the sand and, well, sea water doesn't dry very nicely on denim."

"Ah, the selkie."

"Yes, the selkie needed a bit of help getting back to the sea," I said, straightening and surveying my hooves. The sand hadn't stuck and my furred shins were hidden behind the denim, but I'd stamped them against the concrete porch to make doubly sure I didn't track any inside. "Which I was able to provide, thanks to you."

The smile lit up his handsome face.

Kenan Sagar was a tall hunk of lean muscle and gorgeous looks hidden behind preppy outfits, glasses, and a sculpted beard. Impressive in both stature and physique, he only had a couple of inches on me.

He carried a certain air of vulnerability I found very appealing. Sometimes I wondered if my inner infernal cravings fuelled the need, but accepted I was very attracted to him. Both the demon and the woman wanted to hug him.

I tilted my head and grinned. "Were you waiting for me?"

Kenan looked away, but I spotted the pink on his cheeks. No beard could hide his usual reaction at being teased. A reaction that made me happy because having any kind of effect on this man always gave me a little *zing* of excitement.

"Hey, where's your tail?"

"What?" I swiveled my body at the waist, suddenly self-conscious because I always wanted to look my best around him. "I, uh …" Since my arrival in the human world almost fifteen years ago, I'd been gradually losing demonic parts. "*Hmm.* Looks like it's gone."

"Just like that?"

I shrugged like it was no big deal. "Just like that."

"Anyway, you better get inside." Kenan's eyes shone behind his specs. His body language and anxious energy confirmed he couldn't wait to share the details. "I think your next case involves finding a dragon."

"What?"

"Fire and brimstone spewing from the mouth of a scaly creature with a huge wingspan."

"I don't—"

His laughter and cheeky grin cut off my response.

"You're lying, aren't you?"

He chuckled before saying, "Not lying, kidding around."

"You're hilarious, you know that?" No wonder I'd thought he might be behind the angel query back at the convention. "Hey, did you have someone call me about finding an angel?"

The humour vanished from his face. "No."

"Okay, sure." I pocketed my keys and finally stepped into the house. I watched as he closed the door behind me with suspicion burning in my mind.

I might not live in her house anymore, but Zenda Sagar's home would always be open to me. She'd exposed herself to this forever prospect the moment she found me rummaging through her trash for scraps of food. Vampires weren't the only ones who required invitations to gain unlimited access.

"Seriously, I didn't tell anyone to call you about anything," Kenan said.

I narrowed my eyes. "I'm sure you didn't."

"Des, I have no idea what you're talking about."

"Then what's so important you wanted me to come over right away?"

"Oh, yeah. Right." He put a finger to his lips. "Keep it down. I don't want them to hear you."

"Them?" I finally noticed the murmur of voices coming from the living room, which was strange. Zenda greeted prospective clients out back in the granny flat she'd turned into an office. No one needed to come inside the house because the office was easily accessible from the driveway.

"Auntie's speaking to a prospective client." Kenan sidled up beside me and the book he held brushed up against my arm.

For a moment, I wished it was his hand.

"Who is it? Someone important?" I peeked around the corner but couldn't catch a glimpse. "I suppose it must be, if they're worth inviting into the house. Why did Zenda do that, by the way? She likes to keep the private side of her home away from the office."

"Yeah, but this woman came to the front door and I guess she caught Zenda off guard."

I snorted. "Someone caught Zenda off guard? Come on. That doesn't sound like the woman who raised me." Zenda might be a petite woman with an unassuming air about her, and the flapper hairstyle gave her a vulnerable air she shared with her nephew, but it didn't take long for the strength she possessed to shine through. Spending a few minutes in her presence ensured anyone who thought they might be able to trample all over her realize how wrong they were. And that included me. I wasn't the easiest *person* to get along with, and my untrusting, prickly ways took a long time to soften, but I trusted this woman with my life.

Zenda Sagar meant everything to me. I would give my life for hers, and my soul—if I had one.

"I know what you're thinking, but when you see her, I think you'll understand why Auntie let her in." Kenan's whisper filled the entryway.

"Okay, that doesn't seem strange at all." I peeked around the doorway again and caught sight of our visitor. "Wait a minute." I double-checked to see if she was wearing a penguin suit. "Is that a *nun?*"

"Yes, it is."

"What's a nun doing here?"

Kenan shrugged. "I think you have a better chance of finding out than I do. After all, Zenda asked me to call *you* when I was right here."

The words stung. Not because he knew his own aunt had a bias towards me, but because he felt that way. Kenan should never feel inadequate. He was the best and purest person I knew, and that was in a very literal sense. On rare occasions, I found myself in the right state of mind and could see right into a human's soul. A very handy gift to have in my line of work.

It was also why I hadn't given Oki's husband a second chance. A corrupted essence could never truly be rehabilitated.

I sighed. "Don't say shit like that, Kenan."

"It might make me sound like an idiot, yet she never trusts me with anything but the kind of stuff anyone can find by reading a book."

"No one can find the information we need like you," I said. "How many times have I spent hours scouring through boring texts without finding a single answer and then you come along and find what we need in a few minutes?"

"Stop it," he said with the quirk of a smile. "Stroking my academic ego will get you many things, but won't deter me from what I'm trying to say. Aunt Zenda doesn't trust me."

"That's not true." I tried not to dwell on what I might get for stroking his ego.

"Isn't it?" Kenan turned to face me and even behind the glasses, I could see his bright gray eyes in the darkened hallway. "We both know she doesn't trust me outside the office or library." He pointed at the closed front door. "How many times have you petitioned to let me tag along with you, only for her to kibosh the suggestion?"

"That's because she cares about you." *And because I care about you too.* Kenan didn't know that *I* was the one who'd suggested he shouldn't come with me. It wasn't that I thought him to be a weak link or anything like that, but my personal feelings for him often got in the way. It was selfish and stupid, something I constantly tried to come to terms with but couldn't stop myself from feeling.

Whoever thought of a guardian fucking demon? It was all in the upbringing, I supposed.

His eyes didn't leave mine. "I just want to help."

"And you do, a lot more than you think." I reached out and took his warm fingers in mine and the contact took my breath away. How could he still have this effect on me after so many years of casual, friendly interactions? "If it wasn't for you, I never would've known a selkie's coat could heal them."

Kenan was quiet for a moment as he considered my words. "Don't get me wrong …" He glanced at our joined hands, returned the squeeze. "I enjoy helping out in the research department, I really do. But I want to get out there too. To see all the things you do, and everything I read about on the pages of these books."

"I understand, but it's not as exciting as you think." *Liar.* It was totally exciting. Many times, while searching, or discovering a relic, I'd thought about how much Kenan would love to experience the chase.

"I want to go out there *with you*," he said, and his voice sounded husky. His thumb caressed my palm. "I want to stand beside you."

All I could do was stare back and feel the passion his touch roused inside me. I let his words sink in. This wasn't entirely unexpected because we'd been close for many years, and the way he looked at me made me suspect Kenan felt the same way about me as I did about him. But things were complicated between us. For starters, he was trying to help me find a way back home.

Wherever that is.

Where did I come from? Who was I? And what was I capable of? Allowing my heart to open up to becoming more than best friends could prove dangerous. Besides, I didn't want anything to jeopardize our strong bond.

I broke the stare and cleared my throat. "So …" Why did I suddenly find it hard to speak, to breathe? "What were you reading about before your psychic powers told you I was standing outside the door?" We definitely needed a distraction.

"I, uh, I've found another possible way for you to get home." As expected, the mention of his research changed the mood. Kenan slid his hand out of mine and raised the old book in front of him. This one was leatherbound, had yellowed pages and appeared ancient. I couldn't make out the faded text or illustrations. He lowered his voice, which was how we usually tackled discussing our secret project. We hadn't told Zenda about our covert research because according to her, I was already home.

"Really?" I wasn't expecting much. He'd been trying to find a way back for several years. Since he'd gone off to university to get his degree in parapsychology, demonology, and archaeology. Kenan happened to be an overachiever and very devoted to his ongoing studies. Which was another reason I didn't want to be a distraction and derail his academic plans.

"Yeah, and I think this tome might help with—"

"Destiny, is that you?" Zenda's melodic voice cut through his eager words.

We both stopped in mid-motion and took a step back, as if we were kids caught doing something naughty. She always had that effect on both of us. Zenda might not be our biological mother, but she still made us feel like teenagers under constant watch.

I cleared my throat. "Yeah, I just got here!"

"You better go in there," Kenan said with a tilt of his head. He hid the book behind him and took a step back. "I'll be in the kitchen when you're done."

I nodded because I liked that much better than his usual, *"If you need me."*

"Wish me luck," I said.

"Luck."

I couldn't help but smile before leaving Kenan in the hallway to stroll into the room lined with ancient artifacts. Every inch of available wall was covered with pieces Zenda or her partner had acquired from their many travels all over the world and places beyond. Masks, symbols, sigils, countless canvasses and oddities encased in glass for their own protection. Some for our safety more than theirs.

My gaze fell on my favorite picture of Zenda and Walter. In this particular photo the couple stood outside the pyramids in Egypt after an archeological dig and were smiling. They'd seemed happy together. I'd never met Walter because he wasn't on the scene when I moved in with Zenda, but the weight of his presence lingered. In the tribal pieces on the wall, the bookshelves lining the corridor from entryway to kitchen—everywhere. Maybe Zenda talked about him so much while I was growing up that I'd developed an instinctive reaction I found hard to explain but never told her about.

Any mention of Walter always made her wistful and sad. I'd found her staring at photos with silent tears streaming down her face many times, and loved her too much to cause needless pain. She'd sacrificed a lot for me.

Zenda reached me before I could turn the corner, and her guest remained out of sight.

"Glad you came so quickly." She took both of my hands in hers and flashed a warm and inviting smile. Today she wore a black silky shirt tucked into a brown pencil skirt that reached mid-shin. Ankle boots were on her feet and her face was free of makeup. Yet she still appeared as youthful as the day I met her. She leaned close and pecked my cheek. "How'd you go with the selkie?" she whispered into my ear.

"I've already typed and emailed my report." Sitting in Lady Bug while watching the ocean had inspired me to finalize the incident paperwork and email it back right away.

"That's not what I asked." Zenda pulled back and, even though she had to crane her neck a bit, met my eyes before her gaze strayed to the top of my head.

I ignored her real question because I didn't want to address the glamour issue written all over her face. "She's back in the sea recovering."

"And the one who stole her coat?"

"Let's just say he won't be hurting anyone ever again."

Her eyes widened enough for the disappointment to leak through. "You had to use your power." It wasn't a question, more of a useless statement because we both knew exactly what it meant.

"I didn't have to, simply did. You know how it is." And she did. Aside from Kenan and Mer, she was the only other person who understood.

Zenda's gaze dropped. "Your glamour is weak."

"I didn't bother taking a dose today because I was going to a convention."

"It's important that you take the herbs every morning, regardless," she said. "We can't have people seeing your best assets."

I laughed at her easy compliment because this woman never made me feel like a freak. She'd always made it sound like anyone spotting my horns would be an inconvenience to me, not a horrifying and bluffing experience for them.

"Yeah, but sometimes I forget." This wasn't exactly true. I never actually forgot to take my *meds,* which consisted of a handful of herbs I dry-swallowed every morning. Our witchy friend, Mer Murphy-Blake, concocted the mixture and never failed to add a whiff of sulfur to get my taste buds going. But I didn't always feel like taking the chewy mess. The herbs were a strong glamour to help conceal my more demonic features from even the most sensitive of eyes—my horns, hairy hooves and, until this morning, my tail.

Excluding those pesky features, I was built like a tall human woman.

"About that," I said, letting go of her hands so I could turn around and shake my hips at her. "Looks like my tail's gone."

I felt the light touch of her fingertips along my lower back. "So it has," she said. "It makes the hole in your jeans look odd."

"Yeah, I'll have to buy myself a whole new wardrobe." The truth was, I might have ruined several pairs of jeans and pants by poking holes for my tail, but I'd also kept a lot more intact.

"Anyway, we'll chat about this later. Come along, I need you to meet someone." Zenda grabbed my hand and dragged me the rest of the way into the living room to meet our visitor. "This is Sister Trinity and she has a very special and strange request."

The nun sitting on the couch was draped in her black-and-white ensemble, and a rueful smile was plastered on her face. A rosary hung down the front of her chest. The cup of tea sat untouched on the coffee table in front of her. Although she reflected the epitome of Catholic purity, something about her made my skin crawl.

I tried to concentrate, see if I could read her essence but came up empty. I was spent from my earlier void exertion.

Sister Trinity stood and held out her right hand. "I'm happy to finally meet you." Her tone lacked sincerity.

"Glad to meet you too." I took her cold hand and, a second before pulling away, felt the familiar sting of fire against my palm. I glanced at my skin as I dropped my hand and spotted the telling ash. I rubbed it away on my jeans but couldn't deny what I'd encountered and seen. It was rare to meet anyone who shared my special freakiness—especially a nun—but this was how the hellish recognized each other. The sting of flame and ash residue.

"I'm sorry if I got ahead of myself when I called you earlier," she said.

My mind skipped for a moment. "Called me?"

"Yes, I inquired about an angel."

"Oh!" She was the mysterious caller who'd tried to break procedure and had avoided sharing any real details about her bizarre request over the phone. It hadn't been one of Kenan's jokes after all. "I remember. We got disconnected."

She lowered her eyes as if ashamed. "I'm sorry to say I hung up. I didn't want to intrude."

"That's okay, your query threw me off. That's all."

"Please, Sister, sit down so we can discuss this most peculiar case." Zenda took her usual armchair in front of the chimney.

I settled on the one positioned closest to the nun.

"As I was telling your mother, I need you to locate an angel for the Church."

"So this is sanctioned by the Catholic Church?"

"Yes, it is." A muscle quirked on the side of her mouth and she turned away to focus on the wall.

Interesting. "Who's the angel?" I was intrigued, but skeptical, by her request. What was her deal? Being a demon myself, I didn't begrudge the existence of angels, but everything about this particular nun felt wrong. And it wasn't just the residual ash and sting after we'd shaken hands.

"Her name is Erela and she fell to Earth recently."

"She fell to Earth?"

"Yes."

"Like the alien in that David Bowie movie?"

Sister Trinity's brow wrinkled in confusion. "I don't—"

"That's not important, Sister," Zenda cut in and flashed me a squinty-eyed glare.

I sighed and crossed my legs. When the nun glanced at what should have looked like feet to her, I wondered if she could see my cloven hooves.

"You want me to find a fallen angel?" I almost laughed at the request but managed to keep my amusement in check long enough to add, "I don't think I've got the skills to locate a heavenly creature."

Having the skill to search for the otherworldly and supernatural tokens was one thing, tracking down the complete opposite of myself seemed futile.

"Well, she's not exactly a fallen angel. I mean, she's not Lucifer, if that's what you're concerned about." Sister Trinity shook her head, sighed, and her eyes strayed to my hooves. "She fell and needs to be returned to her proper place."

"The Church can do that?" I sat forward. "Return someone to their rightful place?" How many times had I suggested something along those lines to Zenda? Many, but she'd always claimed the Church wouldn't have the first clue about doing such a thing. I'd assumed she wasn't comfortable bringing the clergy into our lives, but maybe it had been about whether they could be trusted or not. Because this nun was certainly lying.

"I'm not sure how it works," she answered, too quickly. "The clergymen are the ones with all the answers."

"Then why did they send you out for this task?" Her story didn't make sense.

Zenda sat nestled in her chair, hands on her lap while letting me take the lead.

"I'm simply their messenger," the nun said.

"Okay." I doubted that very much. Organized religion distrusted the female species. If a fallen angel happened to be lost somewhere in this country, a priest or some kind of bounty hunter would be the one searching. Not a woman ordained as a nun because her peers didn't think it right to allow women to partake in the equality of priesthood.

"The Angel Erela is one I've often prayed to. She's the protector of children and the innocent." Sister Trinity licked her lips. "It's crucial to locate her as soon as possible, so that the children of the world have the designated protector by their side."

"And Erela is the one who organizes that?"

She shook her head. "Not exactly, but she is their leader."

"It's a similar hierarchy to demons?"

The nun's face darkened and she physically cringed, but, after a moment of glaring at my legs, she nodded. "Yes, I suppose it is. She is one of the many angels who manages the others."

A leader who ruled over their legion. The differences between Heaven and Hell weren't as big as most thought. The two places were mere mirrors of each other and neither was clearly good or evil. Instead, many gray areas existed in between and a lot of the underworld housed progressive types who weren't obsessed with invading mankind. If anything, demons enjoyed toying with humans, which explained why many chose possession as their main hobby.

"How did she fall? Was she pushed?" Trying to lighten the mood didn't affect the woman who was a ball of anxious energy. Sitting this close to her made me feel prickly.

"We're not sure."

"Then how are you sure she's missing?"

"The Church has … contacts. Ways of finding out."

"Right." The sneaky clergy sure had a lot of tricks up their long and secretive sleeves. "Someone got notification that an angel fell from Heaven through the holy grapevine and then decided to send a nun to hire a random PI?"

"You're not random." Sister Trinity sighed and gestured to Zenda. "The Church has hired your mother to help us multiple times."

"That's true," Zenda said with a smile. Her hands were crossed on her lap, which meant she was enjoying my casual interrogation. She taught by example. How many times had I sat and watched her in action before Zenda set me loose on prospective clients? Too many to count. She was a good teacher, a perceptive listener, and I had no doubt she'd already picked up on the same conflicting cues.

"Sagar Investigations is a name the Church values and respects." The nun made the sign of the cross, but her movements were too rigid. As if she'd forced herself to complete an action her arms didn't want to perform. That didn't make any sense.

Zenda nodded her approval.

I uncrossed my legs and sat forward, my hooves firm on the carpet in front of the armchair. "An angel who protects children has fallen from the sky and landed somewhere in this country. Is that right?"

"Yes."

"And you have no idea how it happened or why? Yet someone alerted the Holy See and they want *us* to locate the angel so the priests can send her back to her rightful place."

"That's right," the nun said.

"Did anyone consider she might have jumped?"

A frown etched her smooth face. "Why would she do that?"

"Beats me. Pressure to perform? She was angry with management and decided to quit? There are many reasons, I can't possibly list all of them," I said. "And this wouldn't be the first time this has happened, would it?"

"If you're referring to Lucifer or the Grigori, this situation has nothing in common with what happened with—"

"But how can you be certain?"

Sister Trinity's brown eyes clouded over with a film of white so gradually I almost missed it. I understood exactly what was happening better than anyone. Along with the ivory sclera came the obvious cracks in her mask, causing tracks to mar her pale face. The way she glared at me with those unseeing eyes told me more than any of her words or mannerisms had. She tilted her head, considered me with a wicked grin before turning sharply towards her other shoulder.

The nun jumped to her feet and her body shook as she struggled to step past the coffee table. Her shoulders quivered and she kept her back to us as she headed for the window facing the street.

Yeah, there's definitely more going on with this creepy lady.

I caught Zenda's gaze and raised an eyebrow.

"Are you feeling all right, Sister?" Zenda called in her usual soothing tone. The one she used when trying to calm people down, or during hypnosis. We'd tried plenty of sessions together, hoping to find out how I'd ended up inside a pentagram with no memory.

The nun's shoulders shuddered in a way that confirmed her inner struggle. Then she stopped shaking and stood very still.

"Sister?" Zenda said.

She turned around suddenly, and we both flinched.

"Is everything okay?" I asked.

"Yes." Sister Trinity rushed to the couch. She sat and smoothed out her tunic. "Sometimes, I get anxious and work myself into a frenzy."

I'd met a lot of people suffering from a variety of anxiety disorders, and none went through such obvious and sudden physical changes. She was a lot more than a simple member of the Catholic Church.

Wish I could get a reading on her soul. No matter how hard I tried, the ability remained closed off to me. If I kept trying to force it, I'd get a headache.

The smile never left the sister's face and when she turned her attention back to me, her brown eyes gleamed.

"I'm sorry. Where were we?" she asked in a pleasant tone.

"I was trying to figure out if—"

Zenda spoke over me. "We were trying to get more information about the poor angel. And would like to know what you require of us."

I flashed my mother my own version of a squinty glare and she grinned. She knew as well as I did, that we should push for an explanation from this strange woman. That Zenda was willing to let the nun get away with the interrogation she deserved baffled, but didn't surprise, me.

"Yes, right. I, *we*, need you to find where she fell." Sister Trinity glanced from me to Zenda like a smiling goon. "That's it."

"I think we can handle that," Zenda said. "What's her full name?"

"Erela, Guardian of Children and the Innocent."

"She's part of the Cherubim order," Zenda said.

The nun's smile faltered. "That's correct."

"She's a Cherub?" I echoed. My mind filled with countless pictures featuring chubby babies wearing cloth diapers and ringlets, while lugging around a bow and arrow in toilet paper commercials. "Like Cupid?"

"No." Sister Trinity shook her head. "The Cherubim are guardians." She turned her attention back to Zenda. "I'm impressed with your knowledge because it confirms we did the right thing by contacting you."

"Are these angels powerful?" I asked.

"All angels are powerful," the nun snapped. "But her power lies in protection not offense. If we don't find her soon, someone else might, and there's a growing industry out there that trades in angels and demons."

Zenda and Kenan often warned me about these despicable types, and Mer even shared a few horrid stories with me. This happened to be another reason why I had to wear a glamour. Not just so I wouldn't freak out the average human who didn't expect a horned demon to live in suburbia, or the sensitives who would notice me because of my strong features, but also because of the greedy who chose to trade in trafficking the rarities of this world. And those beyond.

"We'll take the case," Zenda said. "I'll send you an email. You can peruse our terms and conditions. Then have your superiors read over the contract before signing and emailing it back. Send me anything else you think might help and any further questions you have. We've got enough to start an investigation."

The sister pulled a phone from a hidden pocket. "Please, send me the email right away so I can sign and pay for your services."

Zenda cocked an eyebrow. "Right now?"

"Yes, time is of the essence." Her index finger was poised over her phone.

"We require half of the payment in advance and the rest when the job is complete." Zenda stood. "Is that all right with you?"

She shook her head. "I've been instructed to pay the full amount."

"Very well. I'll send you the contract with all the pertinent information." Zenda headed for the side table near the window, where her laptop sat. "Once you sign and send it back, the deal is sealed."

As she typed away, I considered our new client. She'd tried to bypass the correct channels, turned up without an appointment and obviously had a short fuse. None of those qualities sounded pious to me, especially the temporary ivory eyes and the scorch mark she'd left on my skin. The evidence had faded but there was no denying what I'd felt and the residuals she'd left behind.

What was her story? The *real* story?

I watched as the nun's phone dinged and she concentrated on the screen with narrow eyes and tense shoulders, her fingers flying all over like a pro. How many texts and emails did the servants of God draft? Judging by the way she handled herself, a hell of a lot.

"That was quick! Contract signed and payment received," Zenda called from the other side of the room. "We'll be sure to get started on this right away." She frowned. "Wait a minute, you overpaid by two thousand dollars."

"I did," Sister Trinity said. "It's a bonus to cover my only stipulation."

Zenda turned to face her and the distance between them did nothing to hide the rigid set of her narrow shoulders and sudden distrust.

With the deal sealed, there was no going back.

"What stipulation?" Zenda asked.

"I'll be going with Destiny."

"Excuse me?" I sputtered.

The nun lowered her phone and swiveled to face me. "When you head out in search of Erela, I'll go with you."

"I don't think so," I said. "That's not how this works."

"It is this time." The flash of white in her eye sockets shifted to brown and back again.

"I don't take passengers." I questioned whether my imagination was playing tricks on me this afternoon. After all, I *had* conjured up my pentagram in a crowded place and sent a man below. That always took a while to fully recover from.

"The Church insisted on me going with you."

"Your church isn't my employer. Maybe you should've mentioned this before anyone confirmed or signed anything," I spat, and the warm coil of anger stirred inside me.

"It slipped my mind."

I narrowed my eyes. "I'm sure it did."

Zenda rested a hand on my shoulder and the heat of anger faded back into obscurity. Good thing she had such a calming effect on me because my fury did awful things to those who upset me, and this smartass nun knew how to get on my nerves.

I didn't have the energy to summon my pentagram void again.

"It's okay, we can accommodate your request," my adoptive mother and boss said.

"What?" I said, outraged.

Zenda tightened her grip, an attempt to keep me quiet. "We'll be sure to keep you posted about the progress of Destiny's search and when, or if, she'll be heading out."

"Perfect, thank you." Sister Trinity stood and pocketed her phone before making her way around the coffee table. She shook hands with Zenda. "Thank you, we really appreciate your help." When she extended a hand to me, I pretended not to notice the gesture.

One instance of physical contact with the freaky chick was enough.

"I'll show you out," Zenda said, leading the nun out of the living room while glaring at me.

I didn't care if I'd come across as rude by refusing to shake her hand, and I wasn't going to take that crazy bitch with me. Politeness might be important for business, but she'd pushed me too far.

My nerves coiled tight and my limbs felt stiff. I shook both hands out in front of me, and rolled my neck over my tense shoulders. During one particular hard swivel to the left, I noticed the stain on the couch where the nun had been sitting. The unmistakable ashy residue she'd left behind.

Without thinking about what I was doing, I grabbed a small plastic baggie from the stash Zenda kept on the side table and used a sticky note to slide the ash inside. I wiped the excess away and sealed the top, then shoved the evidence into the front pocket of my jeans a second before the front door slammed shut. I knew who could test the ash and I didn't want to tell Zenda about it. Not yet.

"You, in the kitchen, now!" She ducked her head into the living room, scaring the hell out of me.

"Yes, ma'am."

CHAPTER THREE

"You *really* have to learn to control that temper of yours before it causes major havoc," Zenda said. She paced the kitchen with arms crossed, which indicated how pissed off she was.

The tap-tapping of her heels made me cringe because once the horrid noise got into my ears, I couldn't block it out. I wasn't sure why, but I found continuous knocking hard to shake. The pesky clatter made me want to tear the walls down.

I took several breaths before responding. "It's hard."

Most of the time the anger sneaking up on me didn't register until it was too late. It expanded into a huge uncontrollable ball of rage capable of tearing a preternatural hole in the ground.

When Oki's husband took the coat from me and alluded to what he'd done, his vile reaction affected me physically and compelled the violence he deserved. At least, that was what I told myself. How I excused my response without analyzing my actions too closely.

That was Zenda's job, and she hadn't been able to crack the formula.

Kenan sat quietly across the kitchen table and appeared to be as fidgety as me.

"Have you been doing the meditations I showed you?"

"Yes, but meditation doesn't help much." Didn't help at all. Besides, my overactive mind usually stopped meditating early on and I'd spend hours pondering things I shouldn't be thinking about. Like, why would anyone summon and then abandon me like I was a piece of crap? Who would bother to conjure a demon and then leave them without instruction or care? Sure, most demons preferred to pursue their own path, but I wasn't one of them. I was the type who required their summoner's instruction and connection.

I was a child when my summoner abandoned me.

Not for the first time, I wished Zenda had been the one who summoned me because we would have had an even deeper connection. But she didn't partake in the dark arts and would never conjure and dump.

She stopped in front of me. "Are you listening to what I'm saying?"

"Yes, I am." But my thoughts liked to run wild, and I'd end up ignoring everyone around me.

"I'll have to find a stronger means of regulating your anger and stop the fiery manifestations of that awful pentagram void, somehow. Mer has to be aware of something—anything."

"She's already tried." The witch helped us weirdos control or suppress our urges with herbs and potions. Mer had concocted a variety of herb remedies, but none of them worked. She'd even shared some of her magical power with me—even though she didn't like to use magic—in hopes of helping me control the rage.

"I understand, but we have to find a real solution that actually works. We can't have you losing it when you get upset," Zenda said. "And that reminds me, what happened to the person who stole the selkie skin?"

I squirmed in my seat, didn't want to get into it because she wasn't going to like my answer. "Shouldn't we concentrate on the crazy nun?"

"Destiny Sagar, you better answer my question or you'll leave me no other choice but to enclose you in the pentagram of doom."

I flinched. She only used that damned thing for my own safety and protection, but I didn't have to like it. Being encased inside a pentagram circle designed to keep a demon trapped so they couldn't reach out and hurt anyone totally sucked. While inside, the world faded to nothing and left darkness at every angle.

"Well, start talking."

The few times I'd been stuck in what I called *the prison of doom* Kenan sat outside the boundary. He kept me company but also helped my sanity and state of mind. Entrapment didn't bring out the best in the demonic and I wasn't immune to such temperamental moods.

I took a deep breath and made a big show of exhaling loudly.

"Well, while I was waiting for Oki, someone took her coat out of my hands." I didn't add that I'd been mentally transported to the beach while touching the skin because it was too embarrassing. "It turned out to be her husband. He must've followed me and refused to let go. When he started bragging about hurting his wife, I lost my shit and before I knew what was happening, he fell into the floor and I got her coat back."

Zenda massaged her temples. No doubt attempting to keep the inevitable Destiny-induced headache at bay. "Did anyone see you?"

"I don't think so," I lied. "You know how I get when it happens, I'm not exactly aware of my surroundings to—"

"Were there a lot of people at the convention?"

"The usual crowd."

"Which means at least one person most likely noticed."

I tried not to reveal the truth. People definitely saw me, but unless one of those convention goers filmed me, no one would believe their claims.

"It doesn't matter," Kenan said. "If anyone did see her, they'll assume it was part of the show. Isn't that the reason why we choose conventions for public meetings?"

I could've kissed him right then and there for echoing my thoughts but settled for a grateful smile.

"You're probably right." Zenda sighed. "Have you figured out where they go after the ground swallows them?"

"Can't say I've tried to find out." I refused to linger on the consequences of my rage-filled actions. Zenda worried about it a lot more than I did. Dealing with my uncontrollable nature and dangerous habits added stress to her workload, as well as to her spirit. "But I *can* tell you that I got a glimpse of his soul and it was rotten."

Zenda didn't say anything.

"I suspect they're probably transported to some sort of limbo." Kenan to the rescue. "Until we find out exactly where you came from, I'm not one hundred percent on the specifics, but whoever you transport below probably spends time in limbo before a legion nabs them."

"That's comforting." I didn't particularly like doing such a thing, but it was kind of cool. I'd never say it out loud, though.

"Either way, we've got to figure out how to stop it from happening because you seem to be doing it more than usual." She shook her head. "When I adopted you, you did it quite often, but after helping you acclimate, it didn't happen for years. I don't understand why the problem keeps popping up."

"It could be the current political climate," I said, truthfully. "The world is regressing at a much faster rate than anyone expected. Too many things anger me and when I come face to face with a violent asshole, my instincts take over." Part of my acclimation and education to fit in with humans centered on the history of man. People were responsible for a lot of terrible atrocities, so watching this manifestation in the modern world upset me on levels I'd never imagined possible.

Why couldn't humans evolve past violence and hate? While reading about the past I'd found many mentions of demons and other evil. Entities who got the blame for humanity's bad deeds, but man didn't need any help. Men were evil incarnate.

"More reason to make sure we get this under control," she said. "Because you're right, things aren't looking great at the moment and if the world is going to control your moods, we are well and truly fucked."

"Zenda!"

"Auntie!"

We both said in unison.

She was no stranger to swearing, but when she used strong language, the shit had *really* hit the fan. And this made me feel even worse because I always seemed to be at the root of her grievances. She continually denied such a claim, but the proof was in the pudding.

I'm as much of a menace as mankind.

"Stop it, you two." Zenda lowered herself onto the chair between us. "What are we going to do about finding this missing angel?"

"More importantly, what are we going to do about that annoying nun?" I sat back on my chair, meeting her eyes. "There's no way I'm taking her with me. I don't do the ride-along thing. This isn't a community job where I take a civilian with me to see the sights."

"I agree with Des."

"What a surprise," Zenda said, looking at Kenan. "This isn't ideal but she signed the contract and we have to keep our word."

"I'm not taking her." I shook my head, adamant. That freaky nun wasn't getting anywhere near Lady Bug. "Why do we have to keep our word when she didn't?"

"Why does a stranger get to go when I haven't even tagged along once?" Kenan couldn't hide the disappointment.

"Plus, what's the deal with wearing that whole nun garb, anyway? I thought modern nuns wore modest street clothes with a crucifix on their collar." I shook my head. "I remember meeting a nun once and she was dressed like a normal woman."

"It is a bit strange," Kenan added. "The nun shouldn't go—"

"Enough!" Zenda raised her voice loud enough to rattle the windows. "Are you two listening to each other? Do you hear yourselves? Because I do, and all I hear are two petulant, selfish kids who don't like when things don't go their way. And frankly, I'm surprised because if anyone understands that life rarely works out the way one expects, it's you two. So many of the problems you've both endured during your young lives have been terrible, yet you're carrying on about something this trivial."

When she put it that way, I did feel a bit foolish.

I met Kenan's gaze and could read the shame in his eyes but I didn't want to back down. Taking that creepy nun wasn't an option. Not when she'd left a neat pile of ash on the couch that was burning a figurative hole in my pocket because I couldn't wait to get rid of it. I contemplated telling Zenda, but she was already annoyed.

"Tell me you at least noticed she's not quite … right." I could have said many other things, but this was the most important and obvious point to make.

"I did, which is another reason we need to keep her close."

"Keep your enemies close, huh?" Kenan said with a sigh.

"She's an enemy, then?" I didn't want to put a label on her, but if the shoe fit.

Zenda shook her head. "Sister Trinity is not an enemy, but she wasn't forthright. She's definitely hiding things but I'm not worried because no one can better your skill level or instincts. I watched you and read her intentions through your reactions."

"What did you read?"

"The same thing you did—she omitted information and we need to find out why. She's right about one thing, if an angel fell, she's definitely in danger." Zenda had lost all of her irritation. "We can't let anyone get their hands on a celestial."

"What if the biggest threat to the missing angel is actually the nun?" Kenan's sharp attention to detail was a skill we both appreciated, and his observations were usually spot-on. "Leading her to Erela could be the danger you fear."

"While that might be a very real possibility, I doubt she wants to hurt Erela," Zenda said. "I think she wants to find her, but I don't believe it's for the reasons she claims."

"What about the fact the Church sent a nun instead of a priest? Doesn't that strike you both as strange? We all know they don't respect women. Why would they send her on such an important mission? That doesn't sit well with me." I couldn't get past it, because the misogyny of the Catholic Church was actually documented. A religion who once claimed single, independent women and midwives were devil-worshipping witches and burned them at the stake with their cats, or hung them to enforce an unjust point, would never hand over such an important case to a woman. Not even centuries later and *not* to a nun.

"I thought of that too," Zenda said with a nod. "That's why I'm calling the local parish tomorrow to have her story verified. It's not clear if that's who sent her our way, though, because she conveniently left out that detail too."

"We can't trust her to go with Des if we don't even know who sent her or what her motivations are," Kenan said, sitting forward. "Let me look into Erela and I'll get back to you. I don't think we should make any hasty judgments on this case until we have more background info."

"I'll try to slow down my process but I can't guarantee it." After clients provided relevant details, my nature compelled me to start puzzling through the pieces and before I knew it, I'd be at home in my special room trying to pursue whatever needed tracking. The compulsion was too strong and I could already feel the need itching at my fingertips.

Kenan caught my reaction and pushed his chair back with a screech. "I'll get started right away and will fill you in as soon as I can."

"Sure," I said. "Thanks."

"No problem." He gave me a rueful smile before leaving the kitchen, and that reminded me about the ancient book he'd been holding earlier. How he'd mentioned that particular tome might help me find a way home. We'd been sidetracked and I couldn't even follow him to try and get some answers without Zenda getting suspicious.

"He'll be okay, you know."

I couldn't hide the confusion. "What do you mean?"

"You worry too much about Kenan, but he'll be fine." She sighed. "Even if he'll only be truly happy when you both admit how you really feel about each other."

My heart skipped a beat. "We're best friends, he knows how much I care about him."

"No, I don't believe he does because you're both too stubborn to admit the truth I've been aware of for years."

"And what's that?" A lump lodged inside my throat. Why could this intuitive woman practically read me like a book, but had no clue about our secret *Get Des Home* project?

"That you're in love with each other but refuse to broach the subject."

"Zenda, I've got enough on my plate. Do you think you could leave my romantic woes out of it?"

"You're right." A sad smile quirked her lips. "You do have a lot to think about but there'll never be a time when you don't have a full plate. It's in your nature, a part of who you are. You're a natural problem solver and once you catch a whiff of mystery, you can't let go." She shook her head but smiled. "Don't look at me like that, I can tell you're already trying to figure out everything about the nun and the angel. Although you're more concerned about why Sister Trinity is lying, than the possibility of a lost angel."

"That's because angels exist, but I don't believe the nun who's pretending to be a soldier of god."

"You think she isn't a nun?"

"I'm not sure, yet."

Zenda placed a hand over mine. "Well, don't lose too much sleep trying to figure her out. As long as we concentrate on the guardian, the nun will eventually go away. The sooner we figure out where Erela is, the better."

"I think that's my cue to go home and *meditate.*"

"I guess it is." She squeezed my hand and left the kitchen.

Alone, my mind filled with a thousand thoughts.

Zenda was right. Kenan and I tried to keep things on the level and chose denial, but she'd been working her matchmaking skills for years. It wasn't her fault, really. She'd simply read the room and the strength of our emotions so well there was no denying what flowed between us. But like I'd told her, I couldn't waste time worrying about it. Not when a new case had fallen into my lap and I had a new target to chase.

She also happened to be right about my need to solve mysteries. Like a dog with a bone, I couldn't wait to sink my teeth into the marrow of the story.

I stood and regarded the kitchen as a sense of foreboding spilled down the walls thick enough to engulf me. Something wicked was heading our way, or I might be heading into *it.*

The logistics weren't important, only the truth and the destination mattered.

Chapter Four

I'd intended to head home, but at the last minute decided to make a pit stop to drop off the stupid ash I couldn't wait to get rid of. I wanted to get some sort of answer about my suspicions. A nun didn't shed ash for no reason, she didn't suddenly develop a severe case of cloudy eyes and get all twitchy, unless she was rotten on the inside. I needed to find out what was going on with her.

And I still refused to take her anywhere with me.

The door opened before I got the chance to knock, revealing a slim, pretty woman with red curls and a forced smile. She was dressed in her usual tee and faded jeans and her feet were bare. If I didn't know her as well as I did, I might have taken offense at the aloof nature of her reaction when she saw me, but she had a lot on her mind lately.

Mer's life had taken a turn for the supernatural even a witch would never have expected.

"Ah, this is the second time someone has predicted my arrival," I said, trying to lift her spirits with a bit of lighthearted chatter.

"That's because you stomp your hooves like some kind of beast." Mer held the door open and motioned me inside. "Considering what you are, I guess it's totally in character."

"You're quite funny when you try."

"Strange, because I don't feel funny," she said. "I don't feel like much of anything these days."

"Gee, I didn't mean anything by it—"

"I know," Mer said with a sigh.

The flapping of wings and a raucous caw erupted behind me. I glanced over my shoulder and found a big crow on the porch railing staring at me. Her black shiny feathers caught the light

"Hey, Omen." I knew better than to pet the bird, but this familiar appreciated a greeting.

She focused her beady eyes on mine and lowered her head, acknowledging me.

I turned back to Mer. "Your bird is really friendly."

"She's only friendly with people she trusts."

"That makes me feel all warm and fuzzy."

"Why don't you come inside?" she said. "And stop pretending we don't have this conversation every time you come over."

"Sure." To the crow, I said, "See you later!"

I stepped into her house and Mer closed the door. She motioned for me to follow her down the narrow corridor.

"To what do I owe the honor of your visit?"

"Can't a girl just pop in for a social call?"

"A girl certainly can, but that's not why you're here."

"You're too perceptive, and feel things too deeply."

"Yeah, it's an occupational hazard."

Her tone made me feel bad because the weight of what life had dished out seemed to be affecting Mer on a soul-deep level.

"If you need help dealing with those furballs, I'm here for you," I said. "I mean it."

Mer was quiet for a moment before she said, "Is it a glamour top-up you're after? I can see your horns but your tail's gone." She stopped in front of me, ambled around and made a sweep for my backside, her fingertips skimming the air between us. "Hasn't Zenda told you not to walk around with a half-ass glamour?"

"Of course she has! But my tail disappeared somewhere between helping a selkie at a convention and a meeting with a nun."

"Really?" Her fingers were on my lower back, no doubt double-checking my claim. Even with the glamour, if my tail was still there, she'd be able to feel it. "It really seems to be gone."

I whipped her hand away. "Yeah, it's gone. Can we move on?"

Mer focusing on anything but the problems in her life didn't surprise me, so I didn't push. I'd offered my help and that was all I could do.

Zenda taught me early on that while helping people and offering objective advice happened to be a great asset, it was useless when dealing with people who didn't want your help. Or someone in denial. I wasn't convinced Mer was in either one of those camps, but she definitely chose to carry too many burdens on her own.

I continued down the narrow corridor until I reached the kitchen at the back of the house. The top half of the entire back wall consisted of glass and overlooked a beautiful wooded area. It never failed to take my breath away.

"It's not the glamour herbs I'm here for," I said. "I've got enough of those to last several months."

"Really?" She entered the kitchen. "Soon, you won't need them. You'll be a real girl before you know it. Still, that's no excuse to be walking around with such weak cover. Anyone could be watching from a distance."

"Quit worrying," I said. "I took it a few hours ago."

Mer rolled her eyes. "Haven't I told you to take it first thing in the morning so that by the time you step outside you're completely covered? And you don't need to take it daily. My herbs cover you for three days at least."

"Can we forego the lecture? I stopped by a convention and didn't think it was such a big deal." I shrugged and spotted Omen outside, flying high in the sky above the tree line. I envied the bird's freedom to soar above everything and escape the confines of those of us grounded by gravity. I coveted her physical capacity to escape. "But, as usual, you had to make as big a deal as Zenda did."

"That's because we care about you," she said with a sigh. "Do you have any idea what will happen if anyone catches a proper glimpse of you?"

"Yeah, I've heard it all before." People would freak the fuck out and start pointing fingers. Then they'd start shooting, or would try to kill me in some other barbaric way. When the authorities stepped in, I'd be sent to an institution or lab, where scientists would perform a bunch of experiments to try and figure out what I was and what made me tick. That was if the supernatural criminal or hunter types didn't abduct me first.

One thing Zenda and Mer never figured into the equation was me. What I could do to those people if they attempted to grab me.

Oh, wait, they have.

If any kind of hysteria started up around me, we all knew how I would react. Sending a stupid, violent asshole into the pit every now and then wasn't too bad. Mostly. But I couldn't send everyone who reacted negatively to the same place. That would be the epitome of the chaos Zenda warned me about, the reason why she drove herself crazy trying to find new ways to help me gain control of myself.

Maybe they're right and I should religiously top-up my glamour.

Real life wasn't like those *what-if?* episodes in shows. Convention or no convention, I couldn't afford to lag on my responsibilities because there would be no going back.

"I promise to do better," I said.

"Oh good, you're back." Mer stood by the counter with two steaming mugs and brought them over to the table. She placed one in front of me.

"When did you go over there?" I asked. "And when did I sit down?"

She plopped down on a chair and considered me. "You got lost in your thoughts again, and I took the opportunity to whip up our favorite hot beverages while I was waiting."

"Sorry, I didn't mean to fade for so long." I often skipped time because of my thoughts. And after, I wouldn't remember moving during those brief episodes.

"Hey!" Mer clicked her fingers in front of my face. "Stay with me. You didn't come over to sit in my kitchen daydreaming, did you?"

"No, I didn't." I reached into my pocket and pulled out the plastic baggie. "What do you make of this?"

Mer leaned closer and squinted, scrunching her nose. "It's ash."

"Do you recognize it? Is it a particular type of ash?"

"I'd need to touch and smell it to be sure, maybe even test it. But it definitely looks like residual demonic ash." She straightened and took a sip from her cup. Mer always drank strong black coffee. "Where'd you get it?"

"From a nun."

She frowned. "A nun was exuding ash?"

"This nun also had the telltale sting of flame in her handshake and the cloudy eyes, with a bad dose of twitching." I didn't want to make light of the situation, but Mer knew how I liked to tackle things. When I went out of my way to simplify the data, it meant things were more serious than I made them out to be.

"That definitely sounds like a demon to me," she said, taking another sip. "How did you meet this nun?"

"She popped into Zenda's house unannounced and hired us."

"Zenda didn't notice all these obvious signs before taking on the case?"

I shrugged. Although I spoke to Zenda about Sister Trinity's strange behavior, I'd conveniently omitted any mention of the telltale demonic signs.

"You're never going to believe what she hired us to find," I said.

"What does a nun want you to find?"

"An angel." Revealing too much information to anyone else would be sacrilegious and broke many professional rules of ethics, but we often consulted with Mer because of her expertise. She happened to be one of the handful of professionals Zenda had on her payroll, and anything Mer could share about this situation would be greatly appreciated.

"An angel, huh?" She relaxed against the chair. "For a second there I thought you were going to say a werewolf."

"No." I frowned, trying to read her reaction. "Wait a minute. You thought I came over because some quack wants us to find a werewolf?"

She avoided my eyes and drank more coffee.

"I would never do that, neither would Zenda." I sighed. "Your secret is safe with us. We wouldn't reveal what's going on with your family to anyone. You understand that, right?"

Mer put the cup down and met my eyes. "Yes, I do. It's just—"

"You're touchy about the subject and totally paranoid, because even out here on the outskirts of town, you're afraid your secret will be exposed." I shook my head. "Well, we're not going to tell and your magic is strong enough to ensure no one figures anything out. Stop overthinking shit."

"I know, I know, it's just taking a toll." Mer looked tired. "Even on me."

"Like I said before, call whenever you need me. Night or day, I'll be there." I cracked a smile. "Besides, I'm the one who's supposed to have the overthinking problem, not you."

Mer smiled back. "You're right. I'm sorry." She exhaled. "Tell me more about this nun's quest to find an angel."

"A Cherubim, to be precise."

"Really?" Her green eyes sparkled. "Why would anyone need to find a Cherub here?"

"She apparently fell and is lost somewhere in this country, and I've been tasked with finding her." I took a sip from my mug, glad to taste the black tea with one sugar and the right amount of milk. "I was on my way home to do my thing but wanted to run this ash by you first."

"I've never heard of an angel falling from anywhere. Unless we're talking about the well-documented Fallen Angels." Mer picked up the small baggie and held it up to the light, her eyes zeroed in on the contents. "I think we should find out what we have here."

"What can you tell me about angels?"

"Not my field of expertise, really. Just the basics—feathered winged creatures who hold dominion over Heaven but aren't as pure as fiction likes to portray them. They're guardians and warriors, but some are psychotic troublemakers who enjoy meddling in human affairs as much as demons. There are several factions who despise and resent us while others are in love with humans and will do whatever they can to help or seduce." She shook her head. "Sometimes with terrifying results."

"Oh yeah, like what?" Hearing about angelic sins provided a fresh perspective after being exposed to the many cautionary tales about demons.

"Some rape and impregnate women, but not all humans can incubate a half-angelic spawn to term and they die in the process, or give birth to ghostly babies no one else can see. And the ones who do have these babies usually end up in psychiatric institutions, while their children never make it past the toddler stage because their half-formed wings tear their tiny bodies apart. It's horrible and barbaric." Mer stared at the baggie. "But there are the rare exceptions."

"What does that mean?" I hadn't expected the information to be riveting. "Are you talking about the Grigori?"

She nodded. "There's always a woman or two willing to offer herself to a Grigori and because the encounter was consensual, the fetus thrives and grows into a baby who cares enough about their mother to come through peacefully. Some of these Nephilim don't develop wings, so they blend into society."

"And the ones who do?"

"Well …" Mer pointed at my head. "They do the same thing you do."

"Are you telling me there are full-blown winged angel spawn out there in the world?"

"Why wouldn't there be?" She shrugged. "You're a full-blown horned demon and you're in the world."

"Touché." I couldn't believe I'd never considered that. "Have you met any angels?"

Mer squirmed in her seat. "A few, indirectly. I have a contact who claims she got involved with one, and another … well, I don't like to talk about him."

"You sure lead an interesting life."

"Either way, none of those angels have anything to do with a Cherub," she said. "The Cherubim are protectors of children, mostly. So, one falling makes no sense to me."

"What else can you tell me about the Cherubim? Until today, I thought they were ornamental pieces of the Renaissance and cheap ways of selling toilet paper."

Mer's warm laughter filled the kitchen. It made me happy to see some of the weight lift from her shoulders.

The front door slammed and the sound echoed up the corridor.

"Well, well, well, what do we have here?" Tera stormed into the room with an air of confidence. The scent of lavender poured off her, but it couldn't hide the musk lying beneath. "Anyone who can make my wife laugh has a place in this home forever." She glared my way and faked a frown. "Oh, wait. It's you! I take that back."

I snorted. "You're almost as hilarious as your wife."

"Des, I'm kidding. We love you, girl." She smiled before pressing a hand to Mer's shoulder and leaning over to give her a quick kiss on the lips. "What have you got there? It stinks. I smelled it as soon as I opened the front door."

"It's ash," I said.

"It stinks like sulfur." Tera scrunched her nose. "Not as bad as you, but still sulfuric."

"Gee, thanks."

"Sorry, I meant to say, no offense." Tera grinned while twirling the back of her short hair. "Guess I forgot how sensitive you are."

"How'd you go?" Mer asked, staring at her wife.

The grin fell from Tera's face. "We made it all the way around the dog park before Cisco and I started growling and wanted to tear the adorable little throats of every doggie. Isla had to drag us away. Luckily, their humans were too busy talking and checking phones to notice the two crazed wolves masquerading as large mongrels."

"That's an improvement."

"I guess …"

I watched the couple as they spoke about the latest test of wolfy endurance. Tera was as pretty as Mer but her looks were darker—short brown hair, brown eyes and silky complexion. She had the curves of an early twentieth-century movie star while Mer looked more athletic.

Tera had recently been turned into a werewolf and was struggling to get used to the fact.

According to Mer, when Tera's sister Isla got married, Isla's violent ex tracked her down to the cabin where she was supposed to spend her honeymoon. Long story short, Isla defeated the monster but her new husband and Tera were turned.

Mer had a trio of werewolves living under her roof and although she provided a remedy to subdue the beast within, newly turned werewolves needed to let their animal out. Suppressing from the beginning would tear them apart and risk becoming uncontrollable beasts. I didn't envy the precarious situation, but this family's strength and love kept them together.

Mer was a trusted contact of Zenda's and had become a friend of mine, so if she needed me, I'd help however I could.

"Anyway, they dropped me off but should be here soon." Tera met my gaze. "They're bringing dinner. You're welcome to join us if you want."

"Uh …" I shook my head and allowed my thoughts to fade back into line.

"She's having another of her deep thought episodes today," Mer said. "She's been fading in and out. It's because of the new case she's tackling."

"What new case?"

"Never you mind," she said. "We can't reveal these kinds of things to civilians."

"Oh, come on. I helped you with the ash," Tera said to her wife.

"My lips are sealed."

I smiled at their exchange. Not just because they were the cutest couple, but because Mer could always be trusted to stick to ethical guidelines. I never hesitated to fill her in on whatever we were working on because she could be trusted.

"If you two are done," I said, interrupting their conversation. "I appreciate the offer for dinner but need to get home."

"To your big new case?" Tera asked.

"Yes, to that."

She pouted. "Oh, you're no fun. Either of you."

"It isn't the first time I've heard that." It really wasn't. Maybe it was a demonic thing, or maybe I wasn't nice to be around. "And it probably won't be the last."

"I didn't mean to give you a complex," Tera said. "Speaking of that, I'm painting a portrait of you."

"Really?"

"Yep, but I can't show you until it's done."

Mer rolled her eyes. "She won't even let *me* see it."

"No one can until it's done."

I took a big sip from my mug and stood. "Okay, that's my cue to get the hell out of here because I've got stuff to do, things to find and places to go."

"Wait a sec." Mer stood and headed to one of the kitchen drawers with the plastic baggie in hand. She pulled out a small vial and motioned me over. "Before you go, let's see what this is."

I stepped closer and watched as she tipped the contents of the baggie onto a small plate. In the light, the ash shimmered with specks of gold.

"Let's watch for a reaction," Mer said.

Tera sidled up beside me, stood so close my nose twitched from her musky wolfy odor. Did Mer detect the smell as much as I did? And if so, how did she live with it day in and day out, thrice over?

Mer uncapped the vial and poured the clear liquid onto the ash. At first, nothing happened but soon, the ash turned to red liquid. Before our eyes, the liquid morphed into goop and puffed out, swelled and grew like a corn kernel, expanding to become a hardened spiky rock. All the puffy bits vanished until a pretty yellow stone took its place.

"That's lovely," Tera said. "But what just happened?"

"The chemical reaction turned the ash into liquid and solidified into a sulfur crystal." She nudged it with her index finger and some of the shiny bits glowed. "This confirms the ash is demonic."

"Or from a volcano," Tera said with a shrug. "What? My parents took Isla and me to an inactive volcano when we were kids and we saw some of the different rocks on display. This looks exactly like one of them." She met my gaze. "You can ask her if you don't believe me."

Mer rolled her eyes. "Okay, we're either dealing with demonic ash or ash from a volcanic explosion near your mother's house."

Her wife smacked her in the arm playfully. "Tease all you want, but I don't have to be a witchy expert to know things."

"Of course you don't, honey." Mer touched her cheek but Tera headed back to the table and plopped down on a chair.

I tried to hide my smile. "Well, thank you for conducting this very helpful experiment. It definitely answers my question." I made a move to leave.

"Hey, wait, take it with you."

"Are you sure?"

Mer nodded. "The last thing I need in this house is any demonic residue. Besides, ash"—she pointed at the stone—"and rocks have defining qualities. You might be able to find out where it came from and who she is."

"Okay, sure." I caught the rock when she flung it to me. "I appreciate this. A lot."

"You're always welcome."

"And I'm forever thankful." I smiled and tucked the yellow nugget that reeked of sulfur into my pocket. Having the nun's shedding problem confirmed sucked, but I loved the aroma it left in the air and happily let the smell fill my lungs.

I was glad I stopped by without bothering to call first, and I felt comfortable fading into the background while this couple carried on as if I wasn't there. I considered them family, and having Mer on our side comforted me.

"Don't forget, if you ever need help with these wolves of yours, call me."

I caught Tera's eye and she poked her tongue out at me. I couldn't help but laugh as I waved and left the kitchen with Mer trailing behind. She stepped ahead to reach the door before me.

"And don't you forget to take your meds."

"I won't."

"I mean it, if you're dealing with angels and the clergy, I want them to think you're nothing more than a girl with a penchant for freaky occult stuff." Mer stepped close and lowered her voice. "Not trusting the nun is a good idea. Also, make sure she especially doesn't figure out who or what you are, okay?"

"Will do."

"And please"—she took my hand, squeezed and released it—"be careful. If you need anything, don't hesitate to call. The pack might be relatively new, but they're ready to face any threat. I'm no slouch myself."

"Thank you, Mer." I nodded and accepted her honest, and very real, offer. "I'll definitely keep that in mind."

"Be careful!" she called as I walked outside.

I headed for my beloved Lady Bug parked on the curb and spotted Omen in the sky above the house. That bird sure kept an eye on her witch.

"You too!" I called back as I climbed into the car and started the engine. My beautiful vehicle might appear old and rusty on the outside but that was the intention. I'd had the engine fully restored and spent quite a bit of money fixing Lady Bug, but she was worth every penny.

Mer was about to close the door when an all-terrain rolled into the driveway. I waited until the brunette and her husband stepped out holding brown takeout bags.

I beeped and waved as I took off. In the rearview mirror, I spotted the couple heading up the porch and just like I'd felt in Zenda's kitchen, a prickly sense of foreboding tore through me hard enough to shake me to the core.

I reached the stop sign at the end of the street and hit the brake.

No matter what path I took, it would lead to a one-way highway to nowhere.

CHAPTER FIVE

Trying to find someone or something—whether human, monster or object—wasn't the hard part. I had no problem seeking the visions that would direct me to the source of my search. All I needed to enhance the power was the warm glow of candles and my intense concentration.

The ritual was fine, but the after-effects usually took a toll.

I called the experience *mind-soar*, and it filled my skull with visions and locations, caused my skin to scorch. The recovery was shitty, and I'd spend hours scratching at the itchy sections of skin and fur like some sort of junkie.

Not to mention the passing out for hours, or getting horny.

As awful as the hangover could be, every bit of the experience was a necessary part of me. To help complete cases and chase down what or who we needed, but also to remind me that possessing such a power meant my inner strength would help me survive this curse.

I used to wish I wasn't a demon, but the older I got the more I realized that I liked assisting people and finding special objects.

If I hadn't been able to reclaim Oki's coat, she would have died on that shore, along with her baby. She would've become another statistic of domestic violence. One more number to add to the long list. Instead, her selkie skin helped her and would ensure she survived to carry her unborn child to term.

Besides, pushing my limits helped tally up all the powers at my disposal and would hopefully reveal real answers about me.

In the human world, Zenda named me Destiny Sagar because she believed it was her destiny to find me rummaging around for food in her backyard. But wherever I came from, I had another name. I had no idea if I'd been born a lowly minion or a demonic of greater rank, but whoever summoned me, abandoned me in a back alley with no recollection of where I'd come from or who I was. I became a confused and broken horned girl who had to learn how to speak English and adapt to survive in a world that wasn't my own.

As much as I loved Zenda and Kenan and our friends, the question about who I used to be before arriving in this world never faded. The fact a human conjured me meant I must have a name known to man. Humans who dared to take part in such dangerous phenomena were motivated by selfish reasons and needed demons powerful enough to grant their deepest desires.

Here I go again, losing my mind to endless thoughts I have no answers to.

Whenever I discovered a new talent, I texted Kenan so he could add the power to our growing list:

Finding lost things via a mental search.

Lighting candles without need for a flame.

Vision narrowing down to horizontal view.

Seeing into souls.

Able to summon a fiery pentagram leading into a void that pulled people under.

Anger that manifested in violence.

I had no doubt the list would get longer. Or maybe it wouldn't.

After all, I'd had a tail this morning and now it was gone—vanished into the ether. And it wasn't the only thing. I'd had red eyes upon arrival, goat legs which had straightened out considerably, and fur all over.

I took a long sip from the whiskey bottle in my hand and enjoyed the burning sensation the liquid fire sent down my throat and into my stomach. Staying hydrated was important but whenever I did this, I needed an extra buzz.

Before heading up to the appropriately named mind-haven room, I checked my phone.

One missed call from Kenan.

I couldn't believe that Zenda knew about my attraction to Kenan and didn't think it was a big deal. But I still found her observations embarrassing.

Yet neither Kenan or I owed the truth of why we couldn't take things to the next level to anyone. We rarely even shared that reason with each other. Admitting our true feelings could hinder our joint quest to find my home and send me back. Committing to each other and allowing a romantic relationship to blossom would only complicate everything—

provide a distraction we couldn't afford. And if we did pursue this connection and found a way back to wherever hellish place I came from, how could I leave him? Why would I leave? I certainly wouldn't be able to take him with me.

Pretending that a strong friendship was the only emotion between us felt easier and safer. Safer for him or me? I wasn't sure.

Is that why you turned away that one time he tried to kiss you?

Yes, it was.

I'd fooled myself into believing such a lie and often wondered if demons had souls. Or if they were capable of loving anyone. Having feelings for Kenan made me realize that I wasn't a soulless monster. And if I hadn't been created with the ability to love, the people who cared about me had helped me develop emotions.

"Ah, stop thinking about this," I said to the darkened house.

Mer was right, my melancholy wandering thoughts were stronger than usual.

I glanced out the window of my cottage-style home and watched the woods darken during sunset. I liked living in the small house Zenda commissioned for me years ago. It had two bedrooms, a kitchen, bathroom and a small living area. Big enough for me and in the perfect setting. I lived in the middle of the woods, like a demon from a fairy tale.

The thought made me laugh and the cackle echoed around the empty house. Living alone filled me with comfort. I liked having the place to myself and doing whatever I wanted when I wanted, but today everything felt hollow. Empty in a way not even the many books on shelves, or stacked on the sparse furniture and floor, could conceal.

I dumped the whiskey bottle on a side table along with my phone and headed up the wooden stairs, no longer clomping as hard against the floor. My hooves weren't as noisy as Mer made out, but I definitely couldn't sneak up on anyone.

At the landing, I glanced at the room directly across from where I stood. The door was ajar, though I kept it closed. Behind that door was a place even more intimate to me than my actual bedroom.

The thump caught me by surprise and I rushed across the wooden floorboards, pushed the door open the rest of the way and stepped inside.

"Who's there?" The quiet ambience shattered, separated into threads of disruption that caused an itch over my arms.

A sudden shift in the darkest corner gave the intruder away, and the strong scent of rotten eggs confirmed a demonic had invaded my privacy.

"What the hell are you doing inside my house?"

Whoever dared to violate my most sacred area didn't answer.

My heart sped up. The sulfuric stone in my pocket hummed.

I stepped towards the multitude of candles I kept on top of the apothecary cabinet on the side wall. A wave of my fingers lit all of the wicks at once, and the warm orange glow gave the room a dreamy shimmer.

The radiance confirmed my suspicions.

"What are you doing here, Sister Trinity?" Seriously, what the hell was wrong with her? The sulfuric stone in my pocket vibrated like a live wire, reacting to her proximity.

The nun didn't respond.

She faced the far wall, standing in front of the wooden panels. I could see her back covered in the black hooded robes of the Church, and both of her shoulders trembled. She jerked violently and created a double exposure of herself with every motion.

"Sister Trinity, what do you want?" If breaking into my home was part of her personal stipulation, Zenda had to tear that damned contract into electronic pieces so we could wash our hands of this insanity.

The disturbing tremble didn't stop. If she didn't leave willingly, I'd shove her the hell out of my house.

I closed the distance with the intention of forcing her to swivel around. Instead, my hands went through her. She split into three different upper bodies, the trio stemming from the same legs and hips but continually changing as if conjoined triplets fought each other. The nun's inner battle definitely involved a hellish kind of torment.

"You have to help us." Her eerie voice filled the room as she rotated.

I wasn't sure which of the three faces had spoken. One was definitely the pleasant nun I'd met in Zenda's living room, and the other resembled the ivory-eyed cracked version. The third scowled and appeared much older with crisscrossed scars, but seemed as human as the nun who'd roped us into this mess.

"I want you to get out of my house," I said.

"Please … *help*."

I wasn't sure what to make of this and certainly didn't want to deal with her.

Before I could decide either way, she vanished with a shriek loud enough to rattle the cupboards and shelves and extinguish every lit candle. One of the cupboards threatened to tip, but I caught it before it hit the floor.

My breath came too fast as I made my way to the wall where I'd found her. In the sudden dark, the strong scent of sulfur led me to the floor, where I found a small pile of black ash. What the hell was going on? Why did her incorporeal spirit sneak into my house to stand in front of a wall like a possessed freak? None of this made any sense, but it definitely confirmed Sister Trinity had danced with a demon or two.

Unfortunately, Zenda was right. We had to keep this woman on a short leash because whatever she was hiding had to be huge.

The phone rang but I couldn't go downstairs to answer. I was stuck to the spot, my mind reeling from the unexpected intrusion. The nun was suffering an internal struggle, but why? And what did it have to do with me? With us?

I had to deal with this case sooner rather than later. Whatever creepy shit affected Sister Trinity could easily get out of hand, so I needed to get a handle on things.

The fact the annoying nun breached my property's protective wards, set by Zenda and fortified by Mer, made me feel a vulnerability I'd never encountered before.

I took a deep breath, exhaled and made my way to the unlit candles. I studied the mercury charms hanging from a hook. These were the only identifying pieces I'd arrived with. Charms featuring the number one and the number three with some kind of symbol, all dangling from the thin chain that had been wrapped around my horns upon summoning.

What did the tokens mean? We'd always assumed the numbers could be my age, but I'd had my doubts from the beginning. As for the symbol, it resembled a capital H with an M attached underneath, and Kenan suspected it might be part of a bigger sigil. But why was I wearing this peculiar jewelry on that fateful day?

I pushed the questions away.

The doubts and phone calls could wait for later. I needed to tell Zenda about the weird incident with Trinity, but I had a more pressing issue to deal with first.

I took a quick peek at the tarot deck clumsily sprawled beside the scattered rune stones, before grabbing five stubby candles. I placed each one on the floor, sat them on the different points of the pentagram star I'd inscribed in the middle of the room with my blood. I'd also cauterized the symbol with my fire shortly after moving in, and the markings had seeped into the boards. I instinctively knew exactly where each marker was located.

As I stepped over the candles, the five wicks lit up.

I sat in the middle cross-legged and let the comforting warmth penetrate past my skin. I took the small yellow stone, no longer humming, out of my pocket. I didn't usually need to touch or hold personal effects but if I had one, I brought it in with me. Better to have an object to help amplify my intuition. I might not understand how everything worked or where my power came from, but small details solidified the more I performed this ritual.

After placing the rock on the floor in front of me, I pressed my hands against my knees. Wearing comfy shorts and a tank top showed my hairy shins and made the fur shine amber in the light of the candles. I rolled my shoulders and tried to clear my mind while concentrating on the object in front of me, focused all my attention on the sulfur.

I stared for so long that my eyes crossed, but my vision expanded beyond this plane until I could actually peek *inside* the rock instead of *at* it.

I'd expected to see the mundane minerals and chemical composition, but tumbled headfirst into so much more.

A young nun and a little girl faced each other while holding hands. The child's eye sockets were fully white, no iris. The nun's attention was glued on the child as she chanted words I couldn't hear. The girl appeared to be hypnotized and her wide grin tore the skin on both sides. Black blood dribbled down the girl's chin, similar to the gunk the ash had turned into. The nun's attention remained absorbed on the child and she didn't notice what was happening near her feet, didn't see the pool of slick oil spreading.

When the girl spoke to the nun, the woman split in three.

I was psychically pushed out of the vision. I tried to catch my breath while focusing on the familiar walls around me. Unlike the entrapment circle Zenda sometimes put me in, this one didn't rub out the rest of the world. I could find solace in my sacred room, and concentrate on the sigils and runes I'd inscribed on every surface with my own blood to keep me safe whenever I engaged in this process.

But I'm not done yet.

Rock gazing turned out to be a surprise I hadn't expected but confirmed Sister Trinity's sinister condition. Who was the ash-blonde girl? The child had obviously been possessed and the nun was probably trying to help, but instead got herself caught in some unexpected trouble. Was this why she wanted our help? Or was she playing a bizarre game I still hadn't figured out? Whatever it was, I wasn't sure I wanted to play.

During my time in this world, I'd often felt the taint of a fellow demonic who recognized me. Yet, I'd never enjoyed my interactions and banished them quickly. Could I do the same to the nun?

No point in wasting more energy on that freak because I have to find someone.

I closed my eyes and counted back from thirteen. As the numbers decreased, I entered a state of numbness and slowly slipped away. While my mind vacated the premises, my body didn't go anywhere. Still, the sense of panicked inertia consumed me because I hadn't performed the task in a few months.

Usually, I preferred to use proper research routes, but the more peculiar cases required faster action to cut the investigation in half.

According to Zenda, my description of how my mind-soar felt aligned with astral projection. She tried it once and didn't enjoy the experience. She'd found having her spirit flow out of her body, while invisibly tethered, unnerving.

I could relate, but the connection between my spirit and body felt secure. My brain simply opened a door that allowed my consciousness to fly out whenever I needed to. Sending me out through the ether until I tapped into a situation worth exploring.

My head filled with angels. Shiny white wings sweeping behind androgynous beings of celestial light peacefully living in their cloudy haven. On some level, the clichéd vision made me cringe, but what else did I have to go on? My perception was fueled by human imagery. I suspected Hell wasn't all fiery pits and torture, and doubted Heaven was all clouds and harps.

Still, I allowed the angelic purity to fill my mind with a level of goodness I could never attain. According to Mer, many of the angelic couldn't either. I concentrated hard and felt wings beating behind me like Omen's had in the sky. I imagined how it must feel to fly overhead and watch over charges who weren't aware of your existence. I enjoyed being happy in the sky while watching over others when suddenly, I fell from above. I tumbled, unable to get my wings under control, spiraling like an injured bird falling from their nest.

The strangest thing was that it didn't feel like I was watching as a spectator. I *was* the celestial.

My imagination could conjure a lot of different scenarios and whichever was the most accurate usually stood out. I wasn't sure how it worked, but from my own brief demonology studies, many demons were equipped to find things—treasure, people, places. I fit into that category and had added this attribute to the list.

The adopted angelic body fell, and landed on the ground with a hard and loud thump that swept up a whirlwind of dirt. My nostrils filled with it, until all I could do was swallow the grit while trying to catch my breath.

I coughed because my sensitive lungs couldn't process such a harsh intrusion.

"Quick, throw it over her before she gets her bearings," someone said above me.

No, I have to go home. I have so many children to watch over. The thoughts were panicked but had a singsong quality.

A scratchy cover was thrown over my body and my skin burned. Was it a net? And what was it made of? Why did it sting?

My limbs refused to respond but my muscles twitched and whatever was draped over me tore at my wings and forced a gush of blood from my mouth. Until I thought my insides might spill out. Was this because angels couldn't survive in the human world? Or was it whatever this net was made from?

I attempted to lift a hand.

As I was dragged away, I spotted the mess of feathers I left behind and cried for each one. Where were they taking me? What were they doing to my precious wings? If I didn't have them, I'd never find my way home. Everyone knew what losing your wings meant in the Dominion of Heaven.

I tried to mentally shake the angel's thoughts from my brain because the anguish interfered with the process. If I didn't separate myself from her pain, terror, and fear, I'd never get a reading of her location.

Was I at the beach? No, I couldn't hear or taste the ocean. The arid and hot air felt as rough as the grains of dirt scratching my sensitive skin. And the sun in the cloudless sky stung my sensitive eyes.

I wasn't used to this kind of terrain. Only the warriors were adapted to deal with such conditions. Not me, not a simple guardian.

My head hurt and I thought my skull might crack in two.

Her worried thoughts were too much and I had a hard time pushing against them. Separating myself from her.

I pressed my hands against my temples. Not the angel's head I temporarily inhabited, but to my own parked miles away. I screamed when the tearing reverberated loudly and shoved me out of the angel.

No longer outside in the blazing sun and unforgiving terrain, I stood in front of the naked celestial with bloody wings spread out behind her. She was chained to a wall and stuck in some dingy room.

"Help me," she whispered through chapped lips.

"I don't know how …"

"Yes, you do," she said. *"Find me."*

Her head drooped and her body sagged against the chains secured around her wrists. Her ankles were secured as well.

Before I could inspect the area for clues, my body was flung back, and the force stabbed into my midsection.

In the sky, I watched the distance expand between us, but managed to get the coordinates. I knew where this poor angel was held prisoner.

My breath caught in my throat and my lungs constricted, but I was back home, sitting inside my sanctuary with newfound knowledge and the location inscribed on my forearm. The glistening bloody letters were the last thing I saw and memorized before my eyes closed involuntarily and my head hit the floor.

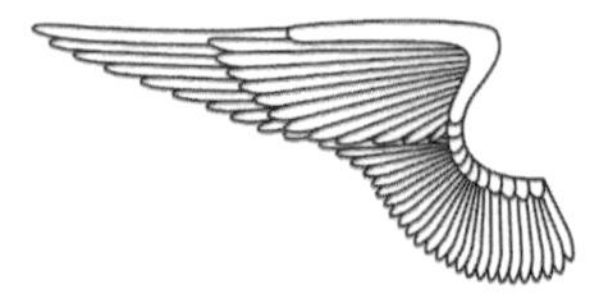

ETHEREAL INTERLUDE

Erela had seen and felt the demon come to her, but she was alone again. Had she imagined the horned woman during her delirium, or did she really visit this cell? She couldn't be sure because no telltale signs remained to determine what was true and what was imagined.

The damage done to her physical shell was as serious as the fragility of her mental state. She couldn't be sure of anything, not since the moment she'd been dragged from her guardian throne.

"Oh, good, you're awake."

She jumped at the unexpected scratchy voice, but couldn't see who had entered the putrid room. She only recognized the juvenile tone, which should have given her hope. After all, she watched and protected children.

"Please," Erela whispered through her cracked and stinging lips. "Let me go."

"I'm sorry, we can't do that."

"But ... I have to get back—"

"Who were you talking to?" the girl asked.

"I wasn't talking to anyone." Lying came with a price for the angelic, but she would deal with that later. The punishment being thrust upon her covered the slip.

"Sure you were." The shadows shifted but the child didn't reveal herself. "I heard you asking for help." She giggled. "But no one can help you. You're ours for as long as we need you."

"I need to watch over the children."

"There are plenty of children here for you to watch over." The girl giggled again. "Soon, they'll nibble on your body and you'll help them in a different way."

Erela recoiled at the words. The memory of younglings with sharp teeth and hollow eyes shook her to the core. These children had caught some sort of pestilence that couldn't be removed by the presence of a lone Cherub, but would have to be eliminated.

"Don't worry, you'll soon find out what your place in our town is," the girl said. "And when you do, you're going to love what we have in store."

"What is it?"

"It's a secret, I can't tell you."

"Can I have some … water?"

"Of course you can." A small pale foot extended from the shadows and kicked a metallic bucket. Water sloshed over the sides, but remained out of reach.

She licked her lips because the liquid made her salivate. "Closer, please."

"I think that's close enough. I better get going."

"No. Wait!"

It was too late. The child was gone, left her alone inside the filthy concrete cage with her arms and legs secured by poisonous brass and a bucket of dirty water she couldn't reach.

For the first time in her long existence, Erela selfishly wished her powers extended to herself. If they did, she might have been able to break the chains and curse the youngsters.

No, you mustn't think like that.

Either way, she wasn't strong enough to do anything. Her authority extended to watchful guidance from above, nothing more.

Erela wasn't sure if the demonic brass staining her skin, or the strong scent of sulfur and brimstone in the air affected her deeper, but the purity seemed to be diminishing by the second. Maybe her captors wanted to break her until she lost herself and joined the league of the wicked.

But she would never submit.

Erela straightened her body and tried to ignore the pain she inadvertently caused her wings because they were trapped between wall and spine.

She prayed that the horned demon could help her.

Erela didn't understand why or how she'd managed to feel the demoniac inside her head and outside her body, but there had to be a reason. Whatever it was, she'd connected to the demonic and if her only way out was to tap into the link, she would.

A manic chuckle escaped Erela when she fantasized about a demon coming to her rescue … surely, she was done for.

Chapter Six

I opened one eye followed by the other. Even such simple and automatic movements took too much energy. I sucked in a breath through my teeth and regretted the action when the sharp pain tore from chest to stomach, making me wonder if my ribs would shatter if I took another. I felt like I was splitting in two and I couldn't do a damn thing to stop it.

Warm tears dribbled down the sides of my face and irritated my delicate skin. My tongue felt too big for my mouth and my gums ached. I tasted blood. Yes, demons had blood coursing through their veins. Maybe mine happened to be a combination of plasma and ichor, more burgundy than red, but we still bled like every other creature.

Take it easy, Des. You know how this goes.

I usually came out of my mind-soar with the hangover from hell, but the effects felt worse than usual. The way my limbs hurt confirmed everything was still attached and would recuperate, eventually.

Sometimes, I woke up numb from the neck down and couldn't move until my body decided to work again hours later.

This is definitely going to be one of those times.

I should have called Kenan to wait this out with me. As selfish as it sounded, he didn't mind hanging out until I could function again. Also, his soothing demeanor helped my recovery, and I liked having him by my side. If I was too weak to walk on my own, he'd carry me to bed so I could sleep off the worse of the effects on the comfort of my mattress. He even covered me with a thick layer of blankets to stabilize my temperature.

Instead, I was lying on the unforgiving wooden floor. Alone. Each slat jabbed into my vertebrae, and I had two especially sensitive spots on the back of my shoulders. I didn't want to think too deeply about the pain because it related back to my angelic vision and the bizarre dream that followed.

Go back to thinking about Kenan …

After he tucked me in all nice and cozy, he'd sit in the chair beside my bed and read until I woke up. Then, would talk about mundane things to make me feel calm.

Kenan, if you can hear me, I need you.

I closed my eyes at my pathetic attempt to get help.

Deluding myself into thinking I could mentally call him to my side like some kind of telepath wouldn't fix the situation.

The search that led to joining with the angel was unlike anything I'd ever experienced during a mind-soar. Usually, I became nothing more than an invisible spectator able to track down a source and take in the surroundings to figure out the location. This time, I'd temporarily *become* the angel and sensed her confusion, pain and emotional turmoil while she fell and was dragged away inside a harmful net.

As if someone had been waiting for her.

Maybe my initial comments about Erela being pushed were correct, but not in the way the nun had suspected. Pushing suggested an attempt to get rid of Erela by literally flinging her off the edge. But what if the action had actually been *dragging*, done from below?

If the hierarchy of angels resembled demons, maybe celestials could be summoned as well. I'd have to get Kenan to look into it.

The phone rang downstairs, but when I tried to sit up, the world spun in front of my hazy eyes. I settled back onto the floor and lay very still.

And what about the strange dream I'd had? The one featuring the angel Erela in chains while chatting to some kid who teased and treated her like shit. Had that really happened? Was I somehow linked to the Cherub, or did my overactive imagination weave possible scenarios to explain what might have happened?

I sighed and decided not to think about it too much.

My body ached and my eyelids got heavier by the second.

The candles had burned down completely and were nothing more than waxy mounds on the floor. How long had my trip lasted? I had no way of checking, not when this room didn't have any windows and I couldn't see outside.

I closed my eyes and gave into the exhaustion.

A voice startled me awake and my shoulders lifted, sending a jitter of nerves from head to toe. Followed by agonizing pain.

"Oh my god, Des!" Pounding footsteps vibrated beneath me. "Are you okay? What happened?"

"Huh?" I opened my eyes and they didn't hurt, but my vision remained blurry. It took several blinks for his face to come into focus. I somehow raised a limp arm and touched his cheek. "Kenan." His name rasped against my dry throat.

"Yeah, it's me." He wrapped his fingers around mine and kept them pressed to his bearded face. "I've been calling for hours and you didn't answer. I was so worried I finally decided to come over."

"Sorry." I didn't say anything else. I wasn't about to tell him I'd attempted to mentally reach him and suspected he might have heard. What kind of craziness would that reveal about me? About us?

"Don't be sorry." Kenan lowered my hand but faltered. He turned my arm and studied my forearm with narrowed eyes. "You got a location?"

"Yes. What does it say?" I thought my brain had grabbed the clue before I passed out but couldn't remember. My mind was as foggy as my vision.

"It says … Hell."

I groaned because it wasn't coordinates. "That's not very helpful."

"Wait a second, there's more." Kenan raised my arm until my skin almost touched the lenses of his glasses. "Where the sand is gritty in the west. Along the highway of the beast. Past the broken shed."

I opened my mouth to answer but instead, my spine jerked as my head filled with the words he'd spoken. I wasn't inside the room anymore, but looking out Lady Bug's dirty windshield as the desert terrain passed in slow motion and the seemingly endless road spread out in front of me. I recognized the spot. I'd been out this far while searching for a missing girl and found her skeleton dumped inside a broken-down shed. That hadn't been the news her family had hoped for, but her parents were able to give her a proper burial and get the closure they'd desperately needed.

"Des, what's going on?" Kenan kneeled close and his face projected over my latest vision. He held both hands out in front of him, as if he wasn't sure whether he should touch me.

My breathing slowed and the desert-scape receded.

I returned to the darkened room.

Kenan propped me onto his lap and I stared into his gray eyes. I wanted to tell him how deep my feelings were for him, but my thoughts faltered. Every jumbled word crammed inside my brain refused to leave my mouth.

The strength seeped out of me.

"I'm going to take you to bed," he whispered before his lips scorched my forehead with a soft caress.

If only he wanted to take me to bed for other reasons, not because I'd turned into a puddle of goo in his very capable arms.

CHAPTER SEVEN

I groaned and opened my eyes, managed to stretch my arms and legs out, curved my spine in a satisfying way that made the bones snap into place. I was no longer a rumpled piece of useless meat on the floor. Though I had an awful taste in my mouth.

The curtains were drawn, but I could see sunlight tracing the edges.

My mind-soar always left temporary side effects in its wake and were a pain in the ass at the best of times. Yet my latest encounter had proven to be the worst one yet. Too many things rushed to the surface. Erela falling. The desert. Her capture and imprisonment. The strange connection between us. An urgency that made me feel like I had to hurry before she was sacrificed.

I wasn't sure why I felt this way, but couldn't ignore what I needed to do next.

My head spun when I sat up and waited until the room settled back into place. I pressed both hands against my head, and rubbed my temples. At least my arms worked and I recognized my surroundings. I was back in my bedroom.

"Whoa, no sudden movements." Kenan leaped out of his chair, dumped the book on the bed and reached for me.

"I'm okay," I said before he could touch me. My skin felt sensitive and his hands anywhere near my body might set me off in a way neither of us were ready for. A situation we might regret, or get a lot of pleasure out of. Maybe both.

"How are you feeling?"

"Like crap." I licked my lips and they were as dry as if I'd actually spent time under the blazing sun in the middle of the desert.

"Where the sand is gritty in the west. Along the highway of the beast. Past the broken shed."

The directions reminded me about the stretch of highway I'd probably have to visit again. Why would the angel be anywhere near a place where I'd made a grim discovery?

I wasn't keen to return to that arid and isolated place, but the sand and the heat didn't bother me. I was, after all, a demonic creature. There might be a lot of weird clichés humans liked to throw around about our natures, but the fire and brimstone were accurate.

"Here." Kenan uncapped and handed me a small bottle of water from the nightstand.

I drank the whole thing in one huge gulp. "Thanks." I made a move to dump the bottle but he took it from me and placed it on the floor instead.

His eyes shone behind his glasses. "You look a lot better." He pressed a hand to my forehead. "And you're not running a fever anymore."

The weight of his palm against my skin made a rush of heat surge in my lower abdomen. I nibbled on my lip. How could I have been close to catatonic and now be consumed with the stirring of lust? The answer was obvious. How many times had I woken up to find Kenan sitting there after my mind-soar recovery and felt the same pull? How many times did I use taking a shower as an excuse to rub one out and let all the tension out of my system?

My condition came with a peculiar side effect. I had the ability to access visions, suffered physical exhaustion afterwards and came out the other end so horny, only an orgasm calmed my nerves and racing pulse. I felt weaker than ever before, and with Kenan here, I couldn't separate my desire from how much I'd promised myself not to cross the line.

He removed his hand from my forehead and straightened. My need for him to put his fingers somewhere else made me twitchy.

"When I found you earlier, you were delirious and didn't look well. I almost called Auntie, but decided to let you sleep it off before taking such drastic measures."

"Thanks, the last thing I need is Zenda fussing over me." Having her anywhere near me after my mind-soaring experience was intolerable and embarrassing. No one wanted their mother to see them in such a powerless state. I pressed my head back against the headboard. "It's part of the process." I glanced at my forearm and wasn't surprised to see the bloody inscription had vanished. My skin was back to tanned, as if words had never appeared like the worst kind of tattoo.

"I get that, but it somehow felt different." His concern softened his features and I wanted to hug him.

I bit down on my tongue, tried to distract myself before talking. "That might be because my latest trip took me into the body of an angel."

Kenan's eyes widened and he sat on the edge of the bed. "What?"

I scooted over to give him room and make sure we weren't touching. Even below the blankets, the pressure of his warm leg would drive me crazy.

"On my quest to find the angel, I somehow embodied her."

"That's amazing," Kenan said. "And we definitely need to add that to your list of talents." He considered me for a moment. "Was it like possessing her?"

"Maybe. I mean, I could see and feel what she was going through. I have to find her."

"I don't think you're ready yet." Kenan shook his head and a strand of hair tumbled over his forehead. "For starters, you haven't had anything to eat."

"I can do that later—"

"Wait here, I'll be right back." He left the room and I heard him running down the stairs and rummaging around, probably in the kitchen.

I leaned back against the pillow, glad I'd regained control of my body. I considered whether I had enough time to self-satisfy before he came back, but it was too risky. If I didn't take care of myself soon, my already fractured mind would get even worse.

Concentrate on what you have to do. Think about "Where the sand is gritty in the west. Along the highway of the beast. Past the broken shed" and what it means.

I needed to make a plan and head out, find this angel and get rid of that crazy nun. I hadn't forgotten about her intrusion, and would definitely push Trinity to find out what the hell she thought she was doing inside my house. I desperately wanted to get rid of the creepy nun with her many secrets but after what I'd witnessed, I needed to help Erela even more.

She might be my supposed opposite, but we'd both been dragged out of our rightful places by an unknown source.

Maybe this was why we'd forged some kind of connection.

See, you're not as randy anymore.

Until Kenan waltzed back into the bedroom all disheveled and cute, holding a big mug of tea in one hand and a plate piled high with jam donuts in the other. My stomach rumbled and a warm sensation spread between my legs.

"Here you go." He handed me the mug with a huge smile and held the plate in front of me.

"Kenan, tell me you didn't go out to get my favorite donuts while I was passed out in bed!" Not only had he somehow heard my silent call for help, but he'd also put me to bed and then grabbed a treat he knew I'd enjoy after I woke up. Sugar was one of the fastest ways to get my strength back. "*You* must be the angel I've been searching for."

His cheeks reddened as I took one of the donuts and he placed the plate on the bedside table. "I don't know about angel …"

I hadn't meant to sound corny, but the muddled effects of my disorienting experience lingered. This was going to be my excuse for anything I did or said inside my bedroom.

The first sip of tea tasted heavenly, but scoffing down one donut followed by another completed the process. My lips were coated in sugary goodness and my stomach sated. Only one other thing had to be satisfied, and if I didn't get to the shower soon …

"Thank you for this," I said. "I could kiss you."

Silence spread inside the room as our eyes met.

Heat rushed through my body. I might end up passing out for a completely different reason because the way he looked at me made my insides twist. All the need and longing I felt for this man was mirrored inside his eyes and my skin itched so much I wanted to be close to him.

I licked my lips. "I'm not going to take that back."

"I don't want you to." He sighed. "I want to kiss you too. It's taking everything I have not to."

"Maybe you should let go of that restraint for once."

Kenan shook his head. "We agreed—"

"We agreed on a lot of things, but rules are meant to be broken." I placed the mug next to the plate and flung the covers off my body. The shorts made me feel self-conscious about my legs. My thighs and knees might have already become human, but the rest was definitely goatish.

"Des, I don't have a problem with the way you look. I think you're beautiful all over. You don't have to hide from me."

I climbed out of bed and he stepped in front of me.

"Are you sure about this?" His voice was low and husky, those gray eyes burning with desire.

"We haven't done anything yet."

Kenan took his glasses off, made a show of placing them on the bedside table before he leaned down and brushed his lips lightly against mine. "We have now."

"I liked it, did you?"

He answered by covering my mouth with his, only this time all the softness of our mutual passion sent us into a frantic pace. My tongue dipped between his lips and when we collided, a zing of heat raced over my skin. I wrapped my arms around his neck and lost my hands in his hair, pressed my body tight against his. He shivered in my arms.

I moaned as our kiss deepened.

"This feels amazing," Kenan whispered.

I pulled back and took my top and shorts off, threw both on the floor and stood in front of him. I wasn't hiding an inch of my body because all of my glamour had completely faded. My less humanly traits—horns, hairy shins, hooves—were laid bare for him to see, all on display, along with my exposed womanly breasts and hips, plus what lay between.

His eyes drank me in, and there was nowhere for his desire to hide.

Without taking a stitch of clothing off, Kenan kissed me again. His mouth left me breathless, but then his warm lips were on my jaw and running down the side of my neck. He made his way to my chest and I sucked in a breath when he nibbled on one nipple before moving to the other. He traced his tongue down my abdomen and kneeled in front of me. His warm breath against my most intimate spot roused a shiver and I spread my legs for him. Propped one up on top of the bed to maximize the sensations.

I shoved my fingers into his hair as his tongue explored and satisfied me in a way I'd only ever fantasized about, but never expected would happen. I cried out in ecstasy and trembled from the pleasure racing over every inch of my body. This was much better than hiding out in the shower by myself.

Kenan stood in front of me completely naked and sporting an erection. I couldn't take my eyes off him, or my hands and mouth. He hoisted me up and pressed my back against the wall.

"Come on, I can't take it any longer," I said. "Do it."

Kenan entered me, and thrilling sparks of sensation ran through my quaking body.

"Des, look at me."

I opened my lust-filled eyes to focus on his.

"Don't look away," he said as he thrust into me.

I held his gaze and clung to his shoulders, tilted my hips to receive every motion in the most satisfying way. My fingers were in his hair again, and caressing the back of his neck as the wall propped me up.

"Everything about you makes me horny." He didn't stop moving inside me. Not even when he snuck a finger between us and rubbed. "I don't ever want this to end."

"Me neither." Such a crazy thing to say but I didn't care because there were no sensical words available when the combination of finger and cock pushed me close to the precipice.

I kept my eyes focused on his while bracing my spine against the wall, and when the orgasm swept through me, Kenan pumped faster. Ground in deep until a growl tore out of his mouth and he slowed the pace.

"Oh, *Destiny*." His face collapsed against my shoulder.

I couldn't help but smile. I'd never seen Kenan lose control, and I liked that he'd lost his cool because of me.

It took him several seconds of heavy breaths before he leaned back and said, "That was … fucking amazing."

"Yeah."

His eyes were shiny as he held me in his arms and his smile widened. He kissed me again, and I wondered if we were headed into a second round.

"Let's go to bed," I whispered in his ear.

Kenan carried me there, and we came together. Over and over again.

ETHEREAL INTERLUDE

Erela's arms and legs were numb. The pins and needles sensation had left her long ago and her mind drifted in and out of consciousness. She could no longer separate being awake from having a terrifying nightmare. Didn't recognize what was real and what was delusion.

Her new existence held only one sensation—pain.

The angel still couldn't reach the bucket the worthless child had kicked closer, but left completely out of reach.

She didn't like to think such wretched thoughts about children, but the ones in this forsaken place were not like the other youngsters on Earth, like the innocents she watched over. She'd lost countless tears for the sick she couldn't cure and the unfortunate ones exposed to evil adults who stole their self-worth and destroyed their futures. She never understood why these poor cursed creatures were made to suffer at such early ages, but at least she had saved some of them.

If the guardians were fast, they could prevent harm. But there were only so many allotted to their care and billions of children. Every passing day, the population of the world grew beyond the angels' control, and she didn't possess the authority to do anything about it.

With her absence, the department wouldn't have the numbers needed and more unlucky kids would suffer fates worse than death because her fellow guardians wouldn't have the access required. Not while she was gone. Not unless someone else stepped up and usurped her role.

"A penny for your thoughts."

Erela lifted her heavy head but the action hurt so much she barely managed to watch the shadows shift across the walls through her eyelashes.

"Please …" It was the only word she could put together. She imagined reaching the bucket, and dreamt she already had. Only to wake up feeling even more parched than when she'd faded into unconsciousness.

"Are you in pain?" The voice sounded different. It wasn't the juvenile girl because this one was deeper and definitely masculine.

"Y-yes."

"I didn't want it to be this way," he said. "But sacrifice is often the way to get what we desire the most." The shadows stirred and Erela thought she spotted the glow of red eyes in all that darkness. "Tell me, what do you desire the most?"

She licked her lips. "I don't."

"You don't desire anything? I find that hard to believe." The shadows danced like smoke, left the scent of brimstone with every move. "Every creature in creation, no matter where they were hatched has desires and dreams, things that make them glad to be alive. A reason to wake up every morning. Otherwise, how would we survive the monotonous grind of routine? All of our lives eventually become an endless to-do list of things we aim to achieve before doom blows out the candle marking our time." The sigh was strong enough to stir her dirty hair and feathers. "Humans aren't the only ones forced to deal with shit they don't want any part of. Are they? You should definitely understand that."

Erela shook her head, or at least thought she had. She didn't want to agree with anything this monster said. Refused to admit he was right about anything.

"It must be awfully hard to lose innocent kiddies on your watch." The condescending tone was far from sympathetic. "Your *boss* promises a lot—protection, love, kindness—yet, you still fail. How many children have perished because you or your precious soldiers couldn't save them? Your failures have provided me access to some of these kids, so I shouldn't be too hard on you."

Erela didn't respond because her weakness slowly morphed into uncontrollable sobs. Tears slid down her face and through the blur, she spied a little one holding up a bowl to collect every tear she cried.

She blinked and the child faded away.

"Angel tears are such a rarity these days," the voice said. "Your kind is much stronger than they used to be. It's a sign of the times, I suppose."

Erela could feel an oily sensation flowing towards her, invisible fingers creeping along the top of her head that dug deeper. The touch wasn't entirely painful, but uncomfortable enough to make her teeth grind.

"Ah, I see you really *are* self-righteous and don't have personal desires. That's very noble of you. But caring for your charges and taking pleasure when you're able to save another kid and ensure they're tucked into a safe bed every night is self-serving in itself."

The creeping sensation slowly receded from her scalp.

"No." The Cherubim didn't possess vanity or a selfish nature and were definitely not corruptible. Other angels might be susceptible to such things but not them.

"You can pretend you're high and mighty all you want, but I'm sure you'll do whatever you can to get your freedom back."

"Please," she spat, followed by a hiccup. "Why are you doing this?"

"It's nothing personal, really." A moment's pause. "I simply needed to conjure a Cherub to make the ultimate offering and secure the position I covet the most. The one I already held but lost for several foolish reasons."

Erela couldn't respond because, while on some level she understood what the voice was saying, she didn't comprehend what he meant. Only a human or demon would forcibly drag another away from their rightful home to use them as a pawn. Realizing there was, in fact, a reason for being here only confirmed the severity of the situation and the realization Erela probably wouldn't make it out of this dingy room alive.

The image of the horned female entered her mind and she wondered if calling out to her was an option. How could she reach her again?

"That's all you need to know for now."

"What … what will you do to me?"

The male voice didn't respond. Instead, the buckles around her wrists and ankles popped and she lurched onto the concrete floor. Her hip landed awkwardly and her skin tore in several places. She didn't understand what was going on or why, but she took a few deep breaths and crawled towards the bucket still in front of her.

It took a lot of effort, but was well worth the struggle when Erela managed to poise herself over the lip and cupped the liquid into her mouth like a ravenous sloth. The warm water contained several dead insects, but she didn't care. She drank until her stomach sloshed and she doubled over, feared she might throw it all up.

"Thank … you." Erela didn't care if they tied her up again. At least she'd been spared enough sympathy to drink her fill of water. Her dry lips cracked and her throat ached, but she didn't feel like every breath constricted her lungs to dust.

"Don't be too gracious yet."

Erela looked up and met an unfamiliar face. This demon, dressed like a young girl with light hair and freckles, had glowing red eyes and held a horned skull in her small hands. Was it a goat or a bull? She couldn't tell because a bucketful of water didn't provide the nourishment to think straight.

"You have such pretty wings." The voice was back to female. The same voice that had tormented her earlier.

The Cherub didn't have a chance to answer because sudden agony shredded her spine and engulfed all her senses. A pained scream tore out of her mouth as she tilted her head back and spotted the chains hanging from the ceiling. The ones with sharp hooks tightly embedded into the fleshy parts of her wings. Pulling so hard she heard one rip shortly followed by the other.

The vibrations tormented her and she couldn't stop wailing.

Erela was yanked to her feet and her toes skimmed the ground. White feathers and blood rained down around her as the purest part was raggedly plucked from her body.

Horned Lady, if you can hear me, please find me before I lose myself completely.

She didn't want to die in this uncaring place and leave her charges unattended. Her need for survival, even in her worst moment of suffering, wasn't for herself.

The next tear of her wings pushed Erela into a darkness she hoped would take her away from this anguished reality.

Chapter Eight

"Good morning," Kenan whispered in my ear, rousing a delightful shiver.

The wonderful sensations he stirred warred with the anxious ones flowing through my mind, trying to get a grip on my mood. I couldn't understand why I felt this way and could barely capture the tendrils teasing an answer. Every thought seemed blurry, as if an unfocused puzzle lay in front of me and my eyes refused to work properly. Like being trapped inside a dream while unable to read a single word.

Only one thought kept repeating … *Horned Lady, if you can hear me, please find me before I lose myself completely.* But whose was it? It couldn't be mine because why would I refer to myself as a *Horned Lady?* I'd been called a lot of things, but never this. The strange thing was, the term didn't feel like an insult. More like a plea for help.

I yawned, and the act helped clear my mind enough to concentrate on the man lying next to me. My stomach flipped at the giddy reminder of what had finally happened between us.

"Is it morning already?" I stretched my back against him, enjoyed the feel of his naked skin on mine. We fit together even better than I'd ever imagined, and considering all the wickedly delicious things we'd done to each other, the only feeling I should be lost in was ecstasy. Instead, a combination of tired and muddled engulfed all the lingering pleasure I'd expected.

After settling into his arms when we were totally spent, I'd fallen asleep but couldn't find the rest I'd craved. Instead, I'd suffered through fitful sleep tossing and turning. Woke up because blood and feathers filled my brain whenever I did manage to drift into sleep.

Horned Lady, if you can hear me, please find me before I lose myself completely.

Something strange was going on inside my head and I didn't like it.

"I don't know," Kenan said before his lips grazed my neck.

I pushed everything out of my mind so I could concentrate on him. I rolled over until we were facing each other. I'd felt a true and strong attraction before, but after taking things to a whole new level of friendship and trust, I didn't want to ruin the moment.

"Who cares what time it is," I said with a smile.

"Exactly." He reached out and untangled the strands of hair caught on my horns. His fingertips caressed the hard surface, all the way to the tip. "They're beautiful." He smiled. "I always wondered if they got in the way when you slept."

"No, the horns never get in the way. The bad dreams do, though."

Kenan lowered his hand. "What kind of bad dreams?"

"I've always had strange dreams about fire and things I can't remember the next day," I said. "But since taking on this case and doing my mind-soar, it feels like someone is invading my dreams somehow."

He furrowed his brow. "Invading them, how?"

Considering we were best friends and I'd shared as much as I could with him for years, I technically shouldn't keep any secrets. But after pushing the friendship to become lovers, seeing each other naked and offering ourselves fully, was it okay to worry him with pesky problems?

I sighed. These were the kinds of fears I'd dreaded would bother me if we got physically involved. Why did sex have to complicate everything when I'd loved him for ages?

Kenan tapped my shoulder, caressed my skin. "Hey, don't shut me out."

"I'm not shutting you out," I said with a shake of my head. "I can't remember what I dreamt but it's left a bad taste in my mouth. All I can remember is pain, followed by white feathers and blood."

Horned Lady, if you can hear me, please find me before I lose myself completely.

He stopped caressing my arm and his eyes took on a vacant stare. If we weren't close, I might have worried but he always got that way whenever an idea struck him or a certain situation clicked. Although maybe I *should* be worried. What could he have possibly figured out from what I'd said?

"What're you thinking?"

His eyes cleared. "While you were passed out after your mind-soar, you kept murmuring about water and brass."

"Water and brass?" I frowned. "What the hell does that mean?"

"Well, water and brass might not mean anything when they're randomly thrown together in a sentence." Kenan paused, licked his lips. "But the fact you added blood and feathers definitely connects the two."

"How?"

"Both of these things relate back to angels."

"Wait a minute." I sat up. "I don't understand how you made the connection." I wasn't an expert on angels, but not knowing such basic information was frankly embarrassing. Considering the weird shit crowding my brain, I should've made the correlation myself.

"When you have background information it does." He rested his head on his hand, elbow perched on the pillow. "Although, it doesn't take an expert to figure this out. Not when your latest case involves looking for the lost angel Erela."

"That scholar brain of yours is worth a thousand suns, I tell ya." I smiled. "Tell me more. How do they fit together?"

"Blood and feathers are obvious. It means the angel is going through some sort of painful ordeal, and that something or someone is hurting her." His gaze captured mine. "Brass is one of the metals demons favor and if used against celestials, will harm and weaken them. As for water, every creature on every dimension requires that to survive."

My mind raced. Between what he'd said and what I'd seen, the puzzle was starting to make some strange sort of sense. "In my vision, I could see out of the eyes of the guardian angel who was dragged from above. She landed on the sand and was taken after they threw a net around her. When I saw her next … she was secured to a wall with shackles on her wrists and ankles."

Horned Lady, if you can hear me, please find me before I lose myself completely.

"That explains the brass—the shackles."

"And the sand relates back to what was written on my arm."

"*Hell.* Where the sand is gritty in the west. Along the highway of the beast. Past the broken shed," he said with a nod.

"She's in the desert." On some level I'd already figured that out, but getting sidetracked by Kenan had done a number on my intelligence.

He nodded. "But what about the word *Hell?* What does that imply? Because I'm certain it's not referring to the actual realm."

I thought about it for a moment. "Hell can be a lot of things—many different places. I'm not sure what it means in this context, but I definitely have an idea about where I have to go. And by the sounds of it, if I don't get out there soon, this angel's going to be in a lot of trouble."

Horned Lady, if you can hear me, please find me before I lose myself completely.

Erela had somehow figured out a way to psychically call out for help, and if I didn't heed the call, maybe I'd get there too late.

"What about the nun?" Kenan asked.

"The nun is another story altogether. I don't believe that the Church sent her." I sighed, decided not to tell him about the weird encounter in my mind-haven room. "She definitely wants to find Erela the Cherubim, but why is another story. I think she's got a personal stake in this."

"Are you taking her with you?" His eyes stared into mine, and I realized I'd never seen him without his glasses for such a long stretch of time.

"That's still not going to happen."

"How about taking me?"

"What?" My mind screeched to a halt, like a vinyl record skipping off the track. I hadn't expected to be blindsided by such a suggestion.

"Take me with you. Let's go on this road trip and solve this case together. Let me help you figure everything out. You know I can." His gray eyes widened, begging me to respond. "I've already done research on Erela, although the information is scarce."

"What did you find out?"

"She's the highest-ranking guardian angel in her choir and without her, the place won't function as well," he said. "That's about it."

"That's not much to go on, is it?" I thought for a moment. "Someone obviously wanted a powerful angel, but why? And they're keeping her prisoner ... how does the nun fit into any of this?"

"Take me with you and we'll figure it out."

I looked at him, couldn't help but feel the hopefulness vibrating off him. He really wanted this, but I wasn't sure. Other couples had to deal with commitment issues involving weekends away or marriage proposals, to commit to a lifetime. For us, it was whether to let this wonderful man join me during a case I had a feeling would lead to a terrible place.

The fact I had to visit the same spot twice couldn't be a coincidence.

When I'd first ended up on that lonely stretch of road—last year or the year before—which led to the shed off the highway, it hadn't been pretty. The missing child was long dead. Would it be too late for Erela as well?

I glanced at Kenan, trying to figure out how he would deal with such a horrific discovery. The child's abandoned skeleton had stunk up the shed, her flesh torn or eaten away by her attacker and the scavengers who followed. He might have lost both of his parents but he'd never actually seen a dead person before.

"I know you can help, and certainly do." I swallowed the lump in my throat. "We're always talking and texting on the phone anyway. If it wasn't for your research and feedback, I wouldn't have been able to solve a lot of cases. But taking you along is another story. For starters, I don't think Zenda would approve."

"We don't have to tell her." He winked.

I didn't like the idea of keeping Zenda out of the loop. What if I let him come with me, we didn't tell her and he got hurt? I wasn't invincible or immortal, but I was hard to kill. I could survive a lot of punishment a man couldn't. No matter how I felt about him, Kenan was human. And thinking about what we'd done and how good it felt clouded my vision. I couldn't stop fantasizing about all the places we could stop for a quickie along the way, and how much fun sharing a motel room would be.

Not getting proper rest would hinder my instincts, but we'd enjoy ourselves … *Stop it. Stop thinking with your lustful glasses on and think about what's at stake.*

"Leaving her out of the loop isn't fair or right," I said. It was already happening. I let my judgment be clouded by my desire to be together. "Besides, how would you research anything without your handy books and the library back at the house?"

"There's a thing called the internet, and I can access that anywhere. Plus, I have a lot of files on my laptop anyway."

Kenan had an answer for everything.

"Some of these places don't have internet access."

He shook his head and laughed. "Look, you don't have to answer right away. I just wanted to put it out there. I've wanted to go with you for a while and I think this would be a great case for our first field trip. A celebration of us."

I didn't say anything because my conflicting emotions grew by the second. My fears consumed me and his enthusiasm was intoxicating.

"Do you regret what we did?" he asked, misreading my reaction.

"What do you mean?"

"Do you regret that we broke our own rules and slept together?"

I reached out and lightly clutched his bearded chin, forcing him to look into my eyes. "Kenan, I don't regret making love to you. Not for one second. Do you have any idea how long I've wanted to fuck your brains out?"

He chuckled. "No, maybe you should tell me."

"For a long time, okay?" I released my grip.

I didn't want to come across as creepy and confess I'd wanted Kenan since the moment we met. When he came over to spend his first summer with us after his parents died and he had nowhere else to go during holidays from boarding school. Befriending Kenan made me realize I did have a heart because it wouldn't stop racing whenever he was around. I hadn't been able to take my eyes off him then, and I still couldn't. Aside from the odd fantasy about some random girl popping into my head, Kenan was always the star of the show. But as our friendship strengthened through the years and we constantly emailed and texted each other, I'd decided not to ruin things by telling him the truth.

We'd crossed the line, and I didn't fear sharing the most intimate parts of myself. I was scared about how much more I would obsess over him. About how many careless decisions I would make now that we were more than friends.

"Yeah, me too." Kenan placed a hand on my hip. "I've wanted to do that for years. But after I tried to kiss you and you pulled away, I thought we'd never try again."

"I didn't want to ruin our friendship. And when you agreed to secretly help me find a way home, I knew it was the right thing to do. A mutual decision."

He lowered his face. "A mutual decision neither one of us apparently wanted."

I laughed.

"I would love to go with you on this trip."

"I get it." I sighed and decided to change the subject. "Can I ask you something?"

"You can ask me anything."

"What made you come over to check on me?" I asked. "I mean, you're very familiar with my process but I doubt you can sense the exact moment I'm doing my thing. So, why did you storm in at that particular moment?"

"Well, like I told you, I'd been trying to call for hours but you didn't answer and I got worried." Kenan met my gaze, held it. "Aside from that, I could've sworn I heard you calling me. Not on the phone, but inside my head." His fingers trailed over his temples. "Yeah, it sounds crazy, but it's happened before."

"If you're crazy, then I certainly am too because I did call out to you. While I was in pain and feeling like a useless lump, I called for you to come to me. Not because I needed to be rescued, but because you're always there for me." I smiled. "I couldn't stop thinking about how cozy you make me feel. And I wasn't wrong, was I?"

"You're not wrong there," he said with a beaming smile. "Also, it's nice to know that you consider my help to be of the rescuing kind."

"Oh, for sure. If this were a fairy tale, you'd be the charming prince rescuing the strong princess. She might not need his help, but it sure was pleasurable when she got it."

Kenan's phone rang from somewhere in the vicinity of the floor.

"You should get that," I said.

"I want to stay inside this bubble forever."

"Me too, but that's not how reality works." I ruffled his hair. "Besides, I'm starving."

Kenan nodded and slid out of bed in search for his phone, while I checked out the hard muscles shifting beneath his skin. When he finally found it in the pocket of his pants, he put the phone to his ear and said, "Hey, Auntie, what's up?"

My heart skipped a beat. I didn't want Zenda to find out we were in bed together. I shook my head at him, hoping he got the message I was trying to convey.

"No, I haven't seen her," he said, meeting my eyes. "I'm at the library doing research."

I gave him the thumbs up approval. My guy sure knew how to fumble his way out of an awkward situation. Then again, the last time he'd been awkward, we'd ended up in a marathon sex romp I couldn't stop thinking about.

"Yeah, sure. If I see her, I'll tell her you're looking for her." He made a face.

I climbed out of bed and stretched my limbs, while being very aware that Kenan was checking me out the same way I'd done when he got out of bed. I had a lot of things to think about, but not before taking a shower.

"Okay, bye." He sighed. "Yes, I will."

I couldn't help but smile at his reaction.

Kenan disconnected and dumped the phone on my bedside table. "Zenda's been calling you all morning, apparently. She wants to talk to you, but told me to give you a message."

"Oh yeah. What's that?"

"She contacted the local parish and several that are farther away, and none have any record of Sister Trinity. No one needs Sagar Investigations to conduct any sort of investigation on their behalf."

"I'm not surprised." The triple image of the nun facing the corner of the room flashed inside my head. "Whatever reason she has for finding this fallen angel, it's personal."

"I agree."

"Does she want us off the case?" I was already in too deep to back out. Whether we continued on Sister Trinity's behalf or not, I was determined to figure out the mystery of the captured angel. I couldn't leave her out there. Even if I made it to that highway and it turned out she wasn't even real, I could at least rest assured I'd done my bit to help a fellow creature in need.

Horned Lady, if you can hear me, please find me before I lose myself completely.

"No, she wants to solve it even more than before." Kenan sighed. "She's convinced something strange is going on and wants to find out what it is. Zenda also tried to get in touch with the nun but her number has conveniently been disconnected."

"She's right, something very strange is going on and I'll definitely get on the case very soon …" I let the thought burrow into my brain. "But first, I need sex, a shower and food. In that particular order." I sashayed my way across the room, swaying my hips for extra effect, while taking slow steps so he could catch every liquid motion of my body. As expected, his eyes were all over me and when he licked his lips, I knew I'd hooked him in all over again. "If you want to join me in the shower, that's exactly where I'll be."

"That's an invitation I'd be crazy to pass up."

I left Kenan standing in the room with an expression I stored away for future reference. A look I'd cherish whenever I was away and needed some cheering up, a positive pick-me-up to focus on.

Before entering the bathroom, the door to my mind-haven room opened and closed. The smell of sulfur gave her away. Had she been watching us? Did she hear any of the things we discussed and all the carnal pleasure we'd exchanged? When I saw that crazy bitch next, I was going to get some answers.

"The water's nice and hot, just how you like it."

I blinked and found Kenan already in the shower stall waiting for me. When did he get past me? Had time skipped ahead again? Of course it had.

"I'm coming."

"That's the spirit!" he said with a wicked grin.

I stepped into the shower and for a while forgot about nuns, angels, and highways.

CHAPTER NINE

"This is—*mmm*—delicious," I said while chewing a mouthful of fried egg.

"Glad you like it. Do you want more?"

"Pile it on, pile it on!" I nibbled on a crispy piece of bacon.

Kenan held the pan above my plate, used the spatula to dish out more delicious food onto my empty plate.

"Thanks!" I dipped a slice of toast into the yolk of another scrumptious egg. "I'd forgotten what a great cook you are."

"I don't get into the kitchen quite as much anymore."

"Why not? You definitely should." I smiled a wide and toothy grin, probably full of egg and bacon bits, but I didn't care. "If you're going to cook up a storm, I'm going to make sure you stay over a lot more because I could definitely get used to this. That's for sure." I saluted him with my mug and took a big gulp of warm tea.

"I'd love to spend more time here," he said. "With you."

My heart swelled. What had I been worried about? We should've done this earlier.

"We have ourselves a deal, then," I said.

After a refreshing shower with added perks, I felt clean and fresh, ready to face whatever this ugly world had to offer. I'd slipped into clean clothes and Kenan picked out some of the gear he'd stored in my closet. We were both looking and feeling great, and he was back to his adorable preppy self: glasses, shirt collar hanging out of his sweater, and crisp jeans.

He placed the pan in the sink and sat at the breakfast counter across from me, pushing the food around his plate with a fork. "I'm serious. I want to spend as much time as I can with you."

I stopped stuffing my face and narrowed my eyes at him. What was he trying to say? Was he hinting at making a habit out of spending the night? Or did he want to chat about taking things further and faster? He couldn't possibly be talking about moving in. As much as I enjoyed tallying up orgasms that reached double digits, I wasn't ready to have anyone inhabit my space. I needed a lot of room to stretch and sift through my never-ending arsenal of thoughts.

"Kenan, what we did was absolutely fantastic. Mind-blowing sex like that should be repeated on a regular basis, so I'd love for you to stop by as often as you like." I ended my speech by shoving more delicious egg and bacon mixture into my mouth.

"It's about more than awesome sex," he said. "Though that's certainly worth keeping in mind."

"What're you trying to say, then? That you care about me? I care about you too. That you want to be together more often? I'm fine with that."

His eyes sparkled. "Us getting together wasn't because you always get horny after your mind-soars?"

A piece of egg got caught in my throat and I coughed.

He rushed over to pat my back and hand me my cup of tea.

When I was ready to speak again, I said, "What … what do you mean?"

Kenan smiled as he made his way back to his stool. "Did you think I couldn't hear what you were doing in the shower?"

"Well, I thought you might have given me enough privacy not to notice," I said. "Assumed you went downstairs, or maybe put some earphones on while I showered."

He laughed. "It's no big deal. It's not like I stood outside the door listening. I stayed in your room reading. Actually, I often went downstairs but still heard you."

"You never said anything."

"I'm a gentleman, I don't go out of my way to make a lady uncomfortable."

Horned Lady, if you can hear me, please find me before I lose myself completely.

There was the thought again. I pushed it aside, couldn't deal with more while suffering through this total and utter humiliation.

"Don't be embarrassed," Kenan said. "I thought it was hot."

"Yes, that makes me feel a lot better." Although I'd be lying if I didn't admit a part of me kind of liked the idea of him thinking about me touching myself.

I lowered my head and concentrated on eating.

"We're a fine pair of liars when it comes to our mutual attraction, that's for sure." Kenan took a quick sip of tea and stood. "But listen, when I was calling you the other night like a madman, I actually had a reason." He made his way to the shelf under the window and ruffled through his bag until he found a familiar book. "We just got sidetracked."

"Is that the book you showed me at Zenda's?"

"It sure is, and it's proving to be quite helpful." He opened the tome at a marked page and stood in front of me. "While I was trying to find a way—any way—of getting a demon back to their rightful place, I found this."

"You found a way to do it?" Excitement and disappointment fought inside my heart.

"Not exactly," he said.

"What is it, then?"

"This." He pointed at a symbol in the middle of the page. Or rather, a sigil.

I dropped my fork and the sound echoed around the kitchen. "Is that what I think it is?"

"Yeah, it's the mark on the back of your left horn."

And part of the set of charms I'd arrived with.

I admired the intricate lines and squiggles of the symbol Kenan had found branded on the surface of my horns. He'd taken a picture, showed me a way to see it in the mirror. We'd convinced ourselves the etchings might be random.

Now, the sigil was in a book right in front of me.

"What does it mean?" I tried to make out the words written underneath but the print was too faded.

"I can't read it clearly either, but the first two letters spell out *Fo*."

"Fo? What's that?"

"Well, I'm not sure yet," he said with a faraway look in his eyes. "It's clearly a sigil and although there are several different symbols attributed to demoniacs, none are as widely accepted as the *Lesser Key of Solomon*. And this is one of those. I have to refer to my texts to find out more, but I'm sure we're on the right track to finding out who you are. That might not mean you're the demon who the sigil belongs to, but at least it would be a marking of the legion." Kenan licked his lips. "As for what's written underneath, it could be nothing or it could be a lot. Either way, I'm going to find out."

I reached up and kissed his cheek. "I can't believe you found information about me in a book!"

"A very ancient book."

"I wonder if that means *I'm* ancient." I stared at him with a grin. We'd always assumed the one and three charms were an indication of my age. I'd had my doubts from the beginning. "Imagine if I am, and you had sex with someone older than you by centuries."

"Well, let me state for the record that sex with an old lady was a great and wonderful experience that needs to be repeated." He lowered his mouth closer to mine but before our lips touched, we were interrupted by a loud thump. "What was that?"

I tilted my head to stare at the ceiling. "Stay here, I'll go and take a look." I'd already reached the landing upstairs when I realized Kenan was right behind me. "Didn't I tell you to wait?"

"Us pesky young guys don't take instructions well."

I narrowed my eyes in what I hoped translated as a warning but, judging by his smile, all it did was amuse him. "At least stay behind me."

"Can't promise that."

If I agreed to take Kenan with me on a case, would he listen to my instructions? Or would his need to make sure I was safe hinder his reactions? I didn't want to deal with that but certainly had to consider the consequences.

When I reached the landing in front of my mind-haven room, the door opened on its own.

"That's creepy."

I gave him another warning glare and cautiously stepped inside but was smashed in the back and sent flying across the room.

The door slammed shut when my spine hit the opposite wall, locking Kenan out. He banged on the door, calling my name and jiggling the handle but couldn't gain access. I preferred to have him outside the room, rather than get hurt before we even left the house.

"You have a job to do," a husky voice called. "Instead, you've been engaging in wicked deeds like the whore of Babylon. Acting as if you don't have more pressing things to do and other places to be."

I caught myself before I slid to the floor and forced my legs to stay steady, hooves were handy for such a feat. "Show yourself, you creepy bitch."

Sister Trinity stepped out of the corner and her white eyes gleamed. Her angry, ghostly head hung in the middle of the room. Her cracked pale face stood out against the gloom, but the rest of her blended into the shadows.

"You shouldn't cast stones," she said.

"Neither should you." Calling me a whore was unacceptable and I refused to take her bullshit when she'd trespassed into my territory. "Sister Trinity, you shouldn't judge others harshly when you're obviously breaking lots of rules yourself."

She chuckled. "I don't have a clue what you mean."

"Breaking into my house uninvited, creeping around and tainting my personal space is enough to prove my point," I said. "That's before considering all the Catholic commandments you seem to enjoy breaking on a daily basis."

"You're pathetic."

I laughed. "If I'm pathetic, why hire me? Why didn't you go elsewhere?"

The nun hissed but didn't answer.

"How do you keep getting into my house?"

Sister Trinity cackled. "You stole a piece of me and brought it into your home, past the many wards and spells, which gave me the access I failed to gain the first time I stopped by."

I glanced at the floor, where the yellow sulfuric stone sat abandoned. How could I have been so stupid? That made total sense. With all the protections around my property, no one with malicious intent could force their way in. *I'd* welcomed her inside, like Zenda did with me long ago. Invitations made to the infernal could never be severed. Not until the entity who'd been invited died or was banished.

"I wanted to find out what you are," I said.

Her demeanor changed and her voice shifted, becoming smooth and melodic. "I'm Sister Trinity, a nun and scholar."

"That's not who you really are, is it?"

"It's who I was." She morphed back into the other version of herself, the broken demon.

Her multiple personality problem was going to give me whiplash.

"What do you want from me, Trinity?"

"I want you to honor your contract and find the angel. I want you to stop engaging in carnal sin with that needy man. I want you to fucking do what you're supposed to be doing!" Her voice got louder with each word, until a breeze picked up around us.

The cabinets rocked and several candles rolled over the floorboards.

"I intend to complete my investigation," I said. "But you have no right to tell me what I can and cannot do, who I get to spend my time with, or when to get started." Best not to tell her I'd already gotten a lead. I refused to provide more information.

"You're a wicked bitch!" She slashed the air and my skin split.

Blood trailed down my cheek and she was suddenly on me, pushing me against the wall and leaning forward to lick the blood from my face.

She closed her eyes and swallowed like it was tasty wine. "Now that I've had a taste, I'll be able to watch over you—always." Her white eyes snapped open and she seemed to glare into my very soul. "If I don't like where you are, I'll kill the human. He's a distraction you don't need. Frankly, I'm surprised he's still alive. Didn't anyone ever tell you not to keep your sex toys alive after use?"

"If you touch him, I'll kill you."

A drop of my blood dribbled from the side of her mouth. "You can try."

"I'll do more than that."

Sister Trinity laughed again. "Just make sure you carry the piece you stole from me with you everywhere, or I'll make him pay."

I shoved her hard, and sent her flying, but she vanished before my eyes.

The door across the room opened and I sagged against the wall.

"Des!" Kenan rushed over and caught me around the waist before I fell sideways. "What happened?"

"Sister Trinity happened, that's what." I sighed and got control of myself. "I'm okay. She surprised me, that's all."

"Are you sure?"

"Yeah."

He let go and surveyed the room suspiciously. "She was here?"

I nodded and took several shallow breaths.

"But how? Your house is warded—"

"I screwed up."

"What do you mean?" Kenan's confusion darkened his features, but I didn't have the energy to explain.

"Don't worry about it, I'll fix everything."

"You're bleeding."

"She's a very strong evil bitch, that's for sure." I wiped the blood away and grabbed the sulfur rock, stuck it deep into my pocket. This part of her had to accompany me everywhere. I wasn't going to risk Kenan's life on the assumption she might be lying.

Hope Kenan didn't notice.

I headed for the bathroom and he closed my mind-haven's door before joining me.

He leaned against the doorway watching. "What's going on, Des?"

I met his reflection in the mirror. "She wants me to get on with the case and stop fucking around. Literally."

"What?" His eyes widened. "She's been watching?"

"Apparently, and she thinks I'm wasting valuable time." I washed the blood from my face with warm water and soap, dried my skin with a wad of toilet paper and flushed it.

"I can take care of that for you."

I shrugged. "It'll heal on its own." I didn't need disinfectant to clean wounds. But I could do with a good dose of bleach to erase the memory of her scaly tongue on my skin.

"What're you going to do next?"

"I'm packing a bag and heading out before this dumb bitch comes back." I stared at him as I answered, hoping he would read between the lines. "And when I'm done with this case, I'm going to fumigate her and eliminate whatever access she thinks she gained over me."

Kenan seemed shocked. "You're heading out *now?*"

What was confusing him about my next move? Maybe it was that he hadn't experienced the nun's wrath for himself, and certainly wasn't aware about her spiteful threats. I couldn't tell him that she'd threatened him directly because he'd definitely insist on coming along.

I leaned against the sink. "No time like the present."

"Are you taking me with you?"

I bit down on my lip and ignored the sting on my cheek. I couldn't stop thinking about what she'd said. Sister Trinity would kill Kenan if he distracted me.

Directly or indirectly, I wasn't going to put him in danger.

If Kenan was with me and the crazy nun had another hissy fit—which she probably would since I had her damned rock in my pocket—she'd have easy access.

I can't let her hurt him.

"Well?" His hopeful eyes made me want to cry.

"Kenan," I said with a sigh. "When I'm out there working, I need to be on my own. It's how I do my thing."

"That's not true." He couldn't hide his disappointment. "You've taken Mer with you before."

"She's a witch!"

"And I'm a weak human who needs to stay home waiting for a call—"

"No, that's not what I mean."

"It's exactly what you mean." Kenan turned away and stormed down the stairs, thumping his feet along the way.

His reaction caught me by surprise. By the time I rushed after him, he was shoving the open book he'd left on the counter into his backpack and headed for the front door.

"Kenan, wait!"

"What?" He stopped with the handle already in his hand but didn't turn to face me.

"What're you doing?" I pointed at his bare feet. "You're not even wearing shoes."

"Isn't it obvious? I'm leaving."

"But why?"

"I need to think things through."

"Think what through?"

"Destiny, you obviously don't want me to go with you and I need to clear my head." He sounded sad and bitter.

I hated to make him feel inadequate.

"But … we didn't finish breakfast." I didn't know what else to say, and came across pathetic and needy.

"I lost my appetite."

Had he lost his appetite for breakfast, or for me? Did my refusal to take him cancel out everything we'd done? A worm of frustration rumbled inside my stomach, forcing a flush of heat to radiate around me so fast it propelled me forward.

"Did you sleep with me because you wanted to get something out of me?" The words tasted poisonous in my mouth. He might be angry about being left out, but I wondered if the pleasure we'd exchanged had come with the hefty price of expectation.

"Is that what you think?" Kenan spun around. "That I came over to seduce you and worm my way into going on a field trip?"

"No, that's not—"

"If you have such a low opinion of me, then maybe you don't know me as well as I thought you did."

I bit my tongue to stop myself from saying anything I might regret. The seconds ticked between us.

"Don't leave," I said.

Kenan opened the door. "I don't want to hold you up."

"You never do—"

"It sure feels like it from where I'm standing."

"Where are you going?"

"I'm getting out of your way."

"Kenan."

He rushed out the door.

"Kenan!" I ran out to the porch, but he'd already strapped himself into his car and had the engine running. "Don't go!"

He didn't hear me, or didn't care, because he backed out of the driveway without a second glance.

Why couldn't he understand that my motivation stemmed from how much I cared about him? Everything had soured because Trinity decided to interfere.

I went back inside and stood in the doorway, well aware of the fiery pentagram spreading on the floor behind me. Aware the void had opened a few steps away and would suck me in if I simply let myself fall.

All I had to do was let go completely.

Not wasting another second, I closed my eyes and fell backwards. The comforting heat ran across my spine and an inviting warm wind stirred my hair, but I didn't fall through or in.

I landed on the floor, and the impact made me flinch.

Shit!

I lay there for several quiet moments before opening my eyes. I got up to lock the door and shut myself off from the world for a bit. Although this house wasn't much protection nowadays.

As I headed into the kitchen to clean up the happy mess we'd made together, a disturbing cackle echoed from upstairs and made my skin crawl. The bitch had gotten her way.

Horned Lady, if you can hear me, please find me before I lose myself completely.

The angel wasn't the only one at risk of losing herself.

Tears left warm tracks on my face and stung the cut, but I didn't care.

Chapter Ten

I tried calling Kenan again, but he didn't answer.

"Hey, it's Kenan here, leave a message and I'll call you back."

Like all the other calls I'd already made, this one went straight to voicemail and as his voice filled my ear the fissure inside me widened. At this rate, my heart would be completely broken in a few short hours. I disconnected before leaving another message because I'd already left him two and was in danger of slipping into stalker territory.

Besides, I didn't want to make him angrier.

I closed my eyes and tried to recapture the lustful stares we'd exchanged, how his face softened when he got close to the edge. But after catching a brief glimpse of the happiest memories, the image shattered into a hundred pieces. His face was replaced with the dark glare of unrestrained anger he'd flashed my way before storming out of the house.

Everything had slipped from happy to devastating too quickly and it made me feel uneasy. That wretched nun ruined our cozy happiness. She'd invaded our newfound intimacy and destroyed all the closeness that came before, which made me realize that Trinity had to be lying because if she'd seen everything, she would've interrupted earlier.

She'd happened to stop by when we were downstairs in the kitchen and probably figured out what was going on. I had no doubt about that.

Where are you, Kenan?

The knock on the window made me jump and my eyes snapped open.

I fumbled and almost dropped my phone but managed to keep a tight grip on the corner of the case. I caught my breath and turned to find Zenda outside Lady Bug. I wound the window down. No fancy automatic mechanism inside this car, it was all about twentieth-century manual labor.

"You scared the hell out of me," I said with a shake of my head, hoping my racing pulse would slow down.

She considered me for a moment and her brown eyes filled with concern. One side of her immaculate short bob was tucked behind her ear, showing off her silver crucifix earrings—the ones she wore when she was worried. I felt like an ungrateful and selfish runt because I hadn't bothered to check up on her. Hadn't even told her about what happened with Sister Trinity.

You're the world's worst daughter. And you can't even use your demonic nature as an excuse.

"I came out to check if you were going to bother coming inside or not." Her eyes burned with concern and I turned away. "You've been sitting in the car for ten minutes."

"Sorry, I've got a lot on my mind."

"When have you not got a lot going on?"

I rolled my eyes. "I put up with enough of that from Mer the other day. I don't need you hassling me about how easily I get caught up in my thoughts." How much time had passed since I'd last left Zenda's house? Back before I'd upset Kenan and he walked out on me after we'd crossed the line we'd drawn in the sand.

"Why did you visit Mer?"

"Can't I make social visits without getting the third degree?"

"Okay, okay." Zenda raised her hands in a show of surrender. "Come on, I need to talk to you about our latest case."

"Actually, I have to fill you in too."

"Good, let's go then." She eyed the bag on the passenger seat but didn't say anything.

I stepped out of the car, pocketed my phone while locking the door and made sure it was in fact locked. I didn't need anyone sneaking into Lady Bug too.

As I headed towards the pale blue bungalow I'd grown up in, I tucked my keys away and a strong sense of nostalgia stirred inside me. I loved the perfectly sculpted shrubbery on either side of the concrete path and the perfume of the flowers in the air. I especially got lost in memories when I reached the top step of the porch and spotted the swing. How many times had Zenda and I sat close together while she read me a fairy tale, or told me a story from her many travels? We would always have plenty of tea and cookies on the side table, and a blanket in case the night settled in around us because we always had a lot to talk about. Her stories were the backbone of my introduction and education to the human world.

She'd crammed my brain with information, and through her I got to know a man I hadn't met. The way she spoke about Walter made him seem so real I often felt his presence inside the house and couldn't understand why.

I'd been a young demon when I first arrived. In demonic terms, a child really, and Zenda had never skipped a beat in preparing me for a world that would never fully understand, see me for who I really was, or accept me. She knew that in spite—or because—of that, I needed to learn as much as possible.

Before leaving the house to come here, I'd taken my herb medication and my glamour should be in full effect. The fact Zenda hadn't said anything was all the confirmation I needed.

Zenda took on a lot when she decided to open her house to me, but she treated me the same way she treated her own nephew.

I reached out for the white railing when a mental picture of Kenan and I sitting on the same swing struck me. We always used to leave a bit of distance between us, usually with a book, and kept our voices low so his aunt didn't hear what we were talking about. He'd been searching for a way home for a while, and the fact that he'd finally gotten a morsel of a clue made my heart sing. Would he bother finding out any more about the sigil after storming out? Or would the anger motivate him to get rid of me?

Thinking that way wasn't productive or good for my sanity. It also reminded me of what a huge betrayal this would be to Zenda. After everything she'd done and what I put her through, how would she take it? I couldn't repay her kindness by leaving.

I often considered telling Kenan to stop searching.

"Are you coming in?" Zenda held the door open.

How long had she been watching me reminisce silently without interruption?

"Yeah." I followed her inside, shut the door, and tried to shake the strange sense of being watched. A thought struck me as we strolled past the living room. The nun had shed ash inside Zenda's house. Did that mean she had access in and out of here as well? Maybe my taking the ash made it easier for her to keep tabs on two houses instead of one.

"You seem to be lost in thought more than usual today."

I entered the kitchen and sat down, remembered Kenan had been with us the last time we congregated in this room. Back when he took my side and offered to do research on Erela.

"Is Kenan here?" I wanted to convey carefree and casual, but was pretty sure I sounded breathy and needy.

Zenda kept her back to me as she filled the kettle and placed it on the electric cradle so I couldn't see her expression. "No, I spoke to him earlier but he said he was researching at the library. I haven't seen him since. Why?"

"Just wondering." I didn't have the energy to explain. I needed to concentrate on the case and fill my mother in on what I'd found out about the nun. "Sister Trinity paid me a visit today."

Zenda spun around with a frown etched on her face. "What do you mean? She popped in unannounced? Frankly, I'm getting tired of how unprofessional she is. After what I found out, I'm starting to regret taking on this case." She shook her head. "I should probably speak to our lawyer to see if we can break the contract."

I wasn't sure how I felt about that, so I didn't comment.

"She didn't bother knocking on the door." I sighed. "She simply appeared inside my mind-haven and told me to hurry up or she was going to make me pay." My hand subconsciously went to the cut on my cheek. "And she wasn't kind about it, either."

Her eyes narrowed. "Did she do that?"

"Yes, she did." The cut had already healed to a pesky scratch.

"I noticed outside, but didn't want to pry." Of course she'd noticed. Zenda was all about the finer details, which explained her impeccable appearance.

Here I was, comfortable in a random black top and a pair of jeans, while she wore an off-white high-collared blouse and tailored pants. She was even wearing high heels inside the house. This woman's individual style was classy and professional. I'd tried to copy her once, but it didn't work out. Hairy cloven hooves weren't suited to high heels and pantyhose. I liked to keep my legs hidden from the public. At least my tail wasn't a problem anymore.

"Concern isn't prying," I said with a small smile.

"That she got past all the wards and into your sanctuary is of great concern and doesn't make any bloody sense." The kettle whistled and Zenda switched off the power, went about filling the mugs with tea bags, sugar and boiling water. She added a dash of milk for me.

"It'll make better sense when you see this." I pulled the yellow stone from my pocket and placed the damned thing on the table. How much more trouble was this pesky object going to cause me?

Zenda came over with the mugs and placed one near the rock, the other in front of her. "Is that what I think it is?"

"A sulfuric stone. It's what the residual ash she left on your couch cushion turned into," I said, afraid of how she might react. "It's why I went to visit Mer."

Zenda sat on her chair but made the transition seem like she simply flowed onto it. "You could've asked me."

"Yeah, but …"

"You like to be absolutely sure because you want to spare me from needless worrying." She shook her head and a strand of ebony hair unhooked from behind her ear. "That protective streak of yours has to end because it does more harm than good. Keeping vital evidence to yourself puts me in more danger than if you'd been straight with me from the beginning. Almost forty-eight hours have passed since she left residue behind and I haven't done a single thing to counteract because I didn't know."

"I'm sorry." Did she say forty-eight hours? No wonder the nun had gotten impatient. I pointed at Zenda's ears. "Is that why you're wearing those? Because you had a feeling things were off?"

"You should've called me, at least." Her mouth was drawn in a straight line and she avoided my eyes. "I kept hearing noises last night and couldn't find anything or anyone. Turns out it was that pesky nun nosing around."

"Does this really give her access to our homes in a physical sense? Even though she cut me, I got the feeling she wasn't entirely corporeal." I shook my head. "She appeared and disappeared too quickly and never used the door." No one could vanish into thin air unless they weren't really there to begin with.

"She can wander in and out as she pleases. Or even cut and bruise and probably toss you and other objects around, but I imagine she's astral projecting. For the moment." Zenda tapped the side of her mug. "She'd still need a proper invitation to physically waltz in."

I catalogued the information.

"I really am sorry. I should've told you." But how could I tell her I'd gone through one of my mind-soars, suffered the ill effects for hours and then got distracted by her nephew? I couldn't spill these admissions for a hundred different reasons. Even thinking about Kenan made my eyes sting. I blinked away the tears before she spotted them.

"At least I finally know. Better late than never, I suppose." Zenda eyed the rock with distaste. "You took that home with you, she gained access and is haunting you."

"That's about right." I took a sip of my warm tea and enjoyed the taste. Zenda made the best cups of tea because she got the sugar content and the steeping time perfectly. Even better than Mer, who was quite good. "She's really pushy and wants me to start looking for the lost angel ASAP."

"And you're carrying that shitty thing around because she warned you to keep it on you or she'll hurt someone you care about." Her stern gaze darkened. "Is that the real reason why you didn't call me?"

She was too smart, this lady.

"Wish I could claim that was my reason for acting like such a rotten daughter," I said, placing my mug on the table. "She didn't threaten you. She's cunning enough to recognize you can take care of yourself and don't need my help." I smiled. "Maybe she can sense that you've gone beyond human boundaries."

In response, the invisible phoenix who shadowed Zenda flared to life behind her left shoulder with a loud screech that rattled the windows. Spark was fire incarnate. Her feathers glowed so brightly I had to shade my eyes with a hand. She was Zenda's protector, a mythological bird she'd discovered inside a cave where a demonic entity claimed an old Spanish treasure had been hidden. Instead, Zenda found a battered and injured phoenix, who she smuggled home and nursed back to health.

In return, the bird bound herself to Zenda and would ensure nothing ever happened to her. It wasn't my adoptive mother's only alteration but the most notable. According to her, spending time with me had lengthened her already long life. I wasn't sure if that was her way of making sure I didn't worry about outliving her by centuries, or the truth, but I took comfort in it.

I saluted Spark and the fiery bird flashed out of existence.

"She's absolutely beautiful," I said.

"She is." Zenda nodded. "But I can't have her showing herself for too long before she inadvertently starts stealing the life force from others."

"Oh, yeah, I'm well aware." I shivered at the memory, could still remember the pain when the phoenix flew too close. How my fire was drawn to hers. If it hadn't been for Zenda, I probably would've become part of Spark that day.

That was the first and last time I got close to one of Zenda's many weird and wonderful non-earthly friends.

"About the sulfur," she said with a small smile. "You're doing the right thing. It's better if she has direct access to you, rather than your home."

"Can she get back in there whenever she wants?"

"Not if the rock or ash isn't there."

"She claims to have free passage," I said.

"I'm not surprised. She's a compulsive liar, and obviously demonic. Have you figured out what she is yet?"

I took a sip, noting how she wasn't pushing me to tell her who the nun had threatened if not her. I had a suspicion Zenda already knew.

"See, that's the thing." I licked my lips. "She's a weird one to crack because there's definitely a devilish quality emanating from her, but I've never seen anything like her before."

"What do you mean?"

"Well, for starters, she seems to be a trio of *somethings* within the one body."

"Could she be fighting off a demonic possession?"

"Maybe ... but I think it's more than that."

Zenda sat forward, resting her chin on her hands. "Like what?"

"This brings me to another reason why I haven't been in touch." I snuck another sip before saying more. "I did my thing. I reached out to try and find the angel."

Her eyes widened and I feared they might fall out of their sockets. "And?"

"I tapped into Erela and found her location: Hell. Where the sand is gritty in the west. Along the highway of the beast. Past the broken shed."

She gasped. "That's where you found the little girl, Rosie."

"It most certainly is."

Zenda leaned both arms against the table. "Why would this case lead you back to that spot?"

"I'm not sure, but that's not even the weirdest bit." I leaned closer and lowered my voice. With the nun's stupid stone sitting on the table, I didn't want to risk her overhearing our conversation. "I somehow tapped *into* the angel. I saw and heard everything she went through—the fall, the pain when she landed, and even experienced what it felt like to be dragged away inside a net."

Memories of pain and blood, white feathers raining down and such deep thirst that I had to sneak in another sip of tea, engulfed my mind.

"You saw all of this during your vision?"

"Some of it. That's how I made first contact." I ran a fingernail along the mug's handle. "And when I try to sleep, she's there. When I wake up, I feel the awful sensation of pain and grief so deeply it almost drowns me. She's locked up and imprisoned by brass. Erela is confused because she doesn't understand why she was pulled from her rightful place. I can relate to that." I took a deep breath, exhaled slowly. "And she called out to me."

"Really? What did she say?"

"Horned Lady, if you can hear me, please find me before I lose myself completely." I sighed, feeling the weight of expectation. "I get why she wants my help, she's desperate. But I don't understand how this happened, or what she means about losing herself."

Zenda was thoughtful for a moment. "You've created a psychic link with the angel and have become her only point of hope. You're right, she must be desperate and confused, seriously hurt by the sounds of it. As for losing herself, if she spends a long period of time away from home, she'll forget."

"Will she stop being a celestial?"

"She'll be like you." Zenda pointed at my horns. "At first, the angel will remain the same physically and most likely retain whatever powers she possessed, but won't keep her memory. She'll forget about her children." Zenda paused for a moment. "The Cherubim only have one purpose—to guard and protect kids. It's their most important duty. Strip that away because of amnesia, and a hollow place will remain inside her heart and she won't understand why. Sure, maybe some days she'll pass a child on the street and feel a sense of familiarity but she won't remember why."

"That's what she means by losing herself?"

"Exactly."

"That part makes sense, but why are *we* connected? Other beings and people in my visions never see me or respond in any psychic way."

"Angels and demons are two sides of the same coin." Zenda sighed. "As much as the scriptures like to preach one is pure light and good, while the other is darkness and evil, that's not true. It's a convenient way to show their audience how good and evil works but nothing about it is real. Both angels and demons have these qualities within. There are many demons who are non-violent and impassive, some have willingly helped humans throughout history, but the Church conveniently conceals such details." She shook her head, as if trying to stop herself from saying more.

I'd heard it all before.

"Anyway, what I'm trying to say is that reaching out to a demon who exists in this world at the same time as she does, means she's strong enough to feel you and somehow grabbed a hold. If she's imprisoned and treated badly, she probably welcomed your presence," Zenda said. "It's why you must head out right away. You have to find out what they're doing to her and why."

"I've already packed a bag and I'm ready to go."

"Good." She dipped her chin in approval. "Let's finish our tea so you can be on your way." She polished off her mug. "I'm surprised Kenan hasn't been hounding you about tagging along."

"He has," I said. "We had a fight about it."

"Ah, that's why you were asking about him earlier and he's not answering my calls," she said with a crooked smile. "You two are absolutely hopeless. Have you considered taking him this once? Maybe to satisfy his curiosity while you get the chance to see if he's actually a good partner in the field."

"No, I—"

"It was *you?*" Kenan stormed into the kitchen with an air of anger that almost blew me off my seat.

"Kenan, were you listening to our conversation?" Emotions warred inside me. I was happy to see him, but angry about him eavesdropping and interrupting without giving me a chance to explain myself.

"I thought you said Zenda was the one who wanted to keep me out of the field trips. But it was you?" He stood close but the way he looked at me made my skin crawl.

"I did say that to Destiny for many years, Kenan."

He ignored his aunt and stood over me. His eyes blazed behind his glasses "You honestly think I'm a weak man who can't handle any sort of pressure, don't you?"

"Kenan, no, I—"

"Haven't I proven how much I can take after what we did?" he spat, so angry he was shaking. "I've read plenty about how the demonic libido works, and the stamina I showed when we were together was more than I'd expected. Surely, if I can match your raging hormones in the bedroom, I'd be able to keep up outside of it."

"Kenan!" I couldn't stand the way he used our lovemaking as a tool. It made me uncomfortable and cheapened everything that made what we'd shared special. "Stop it, please. I understand you're angry—"

"I've gone beyond anger."

"Can we talk about this later?"

"Do you want to keep us a secret, is that it?" he yelled. "You don't want my aunt to know we fucked for hours."

"Okay, Kenan, that's enough!" Zenda pushed the chair back and stood. "You need to get a hold of yourself. You might want to get field experience, but Destiny's right. Acting like an asshole isn't going to get you anywhere."

His chest was heaving but he didn't respond. I'd never seen him act like that before, didn't even know he could exude such rage. When he made a move to step closer, Zenda wrapped a hand around his arm and he stopped.

"Calm the fuck down before I put you in a different kind of timeout," she warned.

Kenan's frantic panting slowed and some of the anger slid from his eyes. What was going on with him? I refused to accept that he'd use sex as currency. Not when we'd been best friends for years. Not when we'd kept our distance because we didn't want to ruin what we had. And not when he'd shown such care during and after our shared intimacy. Something else was going on.

As I watched, his breathing slowed. As if his aunt's touch calmed him. Zenda was a woman with many talents.

"Why won't you take me with you?" His voice was barely a whisper.

His insistence stirred my anger until I felt my own sense of control slip. "Kenan, let it go—"

"I just want to be with you," he said.

Zenda stared at him as if she somehow knew what was going on but I didn't have the patience to ask for an explanation. Too many shitty things were happening and I had to get my head straight to concentrate on my job. The one thing I'd always feared was happening before my eyes. My attention to detail wearing down because of emotion.

"Do you know why I won't take you with me?" I stood and pocketed the sulfuric stone. "Well, how about the fact that I'm scared to lose you? Or that whenever we're together I get distracted and I forget about everything else. When I'm around you I can't concentrate. Whenever you're in the room, all I want to do is be close to you." The pentagram pit opened up between the table and sink. "You consume my mind and I can't think about anything or anyone else."

Zenda gazed down but she didn't appear worried.

"I won't be a distraction," he said. "I'll stay out of your way, and listen to your instructions. I want to help, and I can be an asset out there."

"It doesn't matter what you do, or how good you are. Kenan, to me you'll always be a shiny beacon." I turned to face him, dared to press a palm against his chest. To feel the rapid beating of his heart, but pulled back before he could capture my hand. "And if that's not reason enough, Sister Trinity told me that if you distract me again, she'll kill you."

I turned on my hooves, walked out of the kitchen, and ran out the door as the void I'd created on the kitchen floor sealed behind me.

Both Kenan and Zenda called out for me to stop, but I left without slowing my pace. I jumped into Lady Bug before either had the chance to catch up and wiped away the stupid tears already trailing down my face.

What did I have to do to make him realize how much I loved him? Didn't he understand that the very thought of losing him tore me up inside? I'd never be able to put myself back together without him in my life. The thought of Kenan getting hurt drove me nuts, and after all the weird and serious consequences I'd already suffered during this case, I knew it wouldn't end well.

I sped away from the curb but caught sight of him in the rearview mirror. Kenan stopped in the middle of the road with both arms raised in the air. Waving at me to wait, trying to call me back. But I had things to do and couldn't afford to get sidetracked.

Kenan, I wish you could hear this—I love you.

The next time I peeked in the mirror, I'd put distance between the house and me, and all I found were rows of traffic on the busy road. And Sister Trinity sitting behind the wheel of the vehicle trailing my bumper.

"What the fuck?"

I slammed on the brakes, unhooked my seatbelt and stepped out of the car as soon as I managed to pull the hand brake. I rushed to the driver with rage burning inside me, caused the bitumen to sizzle with every step.

"What do you think you're doing?" I yelled while tapping the window.

Several horns blasted and obscenities were fired at me, but my focus didn't sway from the driver. I needed the annoying nun to leave me the fuck alone.

When the window slid down, it wasn't a nun staring back. A woman with long, straight dark hair, a white headband, and a confused expression on her face stared back at me.

"Can I help you?" she asked, fear edging her voice.

"I ... uh." This wasn't Sister Trinity. She'd pushed me to the verge of losing my shit and that wasn't safe for anyone. Especially considering my flammable emotions.

"I don't want any trouble."

"Uh …"

She furrowed her brow. "Is everything all right?"

I focused on the woman. "Yes, I'm sorry, I thought you were someone else."

"Hurry the fuck up, you bitch!" I ignored the yelling from the other motorists.

Before the woman could say anything else, I rushed back to Lady Bug and tried not to pay any attention to the black blur I caught from the side of my eye. I climbed into the driver's seat and took off when the light turned green.

I squeezed my hands around the steering wheel and sighed, while trying to stop myself from shaking. Too many emotions fought to consume me, and if I allowed every ounce of uncertainty and doubt to take over, things would not be pretty.

Zenda always feared I might one day lose my shit so badly that I'd push unsuspecting and innocent bystanders into the abyss.

No, I can't allow that to happen.

I drove on and took deep breaths of the sulfur clinging to me. As much as it pained me, I hardened my heart and decided to concentrate on nothing but business. Too much was at stake and I couldn't afford another repeat of what happened because my control was teetering too close to the precipice of darkness.

You can do this.

I've done this before. It shouldn't be hard to get back into the swing of things.

Being on the road would help me stay on target, because that put me back in the driver's seat, and I knew my destination.

The phone rang but I ignored it, even though Zenda's dial tone filled the car.

CHAPTER ELEVEN

By the time I made a pit stop into a gas station to fill the tank for the road trip ahead, I had six missed calls from Kenan and three from Zenda. She'd also left one voicemail message.

I'd reached the outskirts of town by late afternoon. The long stretch of highway was within reach. I looked forward to the endless horizon, the desolate terrain, and the odd truck as company.

I couldn't wait to wind down the window, crank the stereo and speed down the highway. I wanted to let the wind tear through my hair, and didn't care if the long strands tangled around my horns. I needed my mind to wander in every direction without being reminded about the dangers of losing myself inside my head. What was wrong with thinking? Or overthinking? If not for these particular skills, I wouldn't have successfully worked through the majority of our cases.

I needed to embrace the comfortable abandon of useless thoughts without feeling guilty about it for once.

Before I could do that, I listened to Zenda's message:

"Destiny, honey, I hope you're okay, and wanted to tell you that I understand why you walked out. I don't blame you after Kenan's shameful display. But don't worry, I'm going to set him straight. He wasn't himself. The anger and his recent interactions with you must've combined to make a volatile cocktail. It's not your fault and it's not his either, I always knew you two would make an explosive combination." She paused, and sighed. *"Anyway, I forgot to tell you that Sister Trinity doesn't appear to have any affiliation with any of the churches I contacted. Actually, she doesn't seem to be listed anywhere. It almost feels like no one wants to admit that they're associated with her.*

Be careful and don't trust her. I have no doubt, you'll run into her during your travels. And don't worry about us. Go and save the angel. We'll be here when you get back, but if you want to text or call, you know where I am. Love you, my beautiful girl."

Tears blurred my vision and I lowered the phone. Zenda always knew how to say the right thing without coming across as condescending or overbearing. She cared a lot and I'd be forever grateful for her help, encouragement, and love.

I sent her a quick text back: *Thanks. Will keep you posted. Love you Mum.*

A red love heart was her instant reply.

I ran my thumb over the screen and considered whether to send Kenan a message. If Zenda was right and being around me affected her physically and mentally, it made sense that sexual intimacy would feed Kenan my influence on a much higher, more concentrated level. I lost my temper quickly when things didn't go my way, which might explain Kenan's uncharacteristic rage after I'd turned down his offer to come with me.

The only thing that came to mind was: *I'm sorry. I love you. xxx*

I sent the text but he didn't respond.

As long as Kenan knew how much he meant to me, that was all that mattered.

The phobia of keeping him away from fieldwork was an issue *I* had to work through on my own. I'd already added it to my thinking pile because my fears weren't worth losing him. And I never wanted to see him as worked up as he'd become when he'd stormed into Zenda's house. The thought roused a shiver down my spine and made me wince at the memory.

I dumped the phone in the center console and got out of the car.

After filling up the fuel tank and paying the ridiculous amount required to keep Lady Bug on the road, I bought a bottle of water and two chocolate bars. I tried to get a reading on the tired clerk's soul but failed miserably. I wasn't sure what was going on with *that*, but had a feeling my inability had nothing to do with my state of mind and more to do with the swift shedding of demonic abilities.

I'd already polished off both bars when I climbed back into my car, and drank the majority of the water before turning the key in the ignition.

I listened to Lady Bug rattle and roll.

My car might be noisy but she was a beauty. A friendly and helpful vehicle, always a pleasure to drive. Plus she didn't talk back, or hassled me about losing myself in the Great Land of Thoughts. Actually, she encouraged it. I'd come up with some of my best ideas and figured out plenty of shit while driving my lovely beast.

I clicked my seatbelt on and ran a hand over the dash. I was about to take the handbrake off when the passenger door opened and I watched, dumbfounded, as Sister Trinity settled into the seat with her black tunic flying every which way.

"What the fuck do you think you're doing?"

She slammed the door shut. "Watch your language." The nun buckled herself in.

"Get the fuck out of my car. How's that for language, you freak?"

"I said—"

I palmed the underside of her jaw and her head slammed against the window.

"Ouch," she said, while rubbing her face. "What did you do that for?"

"Just wanted to make sure you're actually here."

"You could've asked."

"Nah, I like the hands-on approach." I didn't take my eyes off the suspicious nun because I didn't trust the bitch. I attempted to get a reading on her essence but failed. With her, it could be because she didn't have one. "Besides, you totally deserved that. I owed you one."

"Owed me one for what?"

"Are you serious?" I pointed at my face, at the fading mark. "Did you forget about this?"

She frowned. "I didn't … That wasn't—"

A van beeped and the sound rumbled inside my skull. My instincts had kicked into overdrive. I was aware of every blade of grass swaying swiftly in the wind by the side of the road, the birds flying overhead searching for scraps, and the many cars and trucks inside the station, as well as the ones zooming up and down the highway on their way to new places or glad to be heading home.

I waved into the rearview before taking off, only to stop near the air pumps.

"Why are you stopping?" Trinity asked suspiciously.

"I need to pump some air into my tires." I jumped out and stood near Lady Bug's rump, watching her through the back window. The sister didn't shimmer and shake, or try to touch anything, she simply sat rigid on the seat still buckled in. She didn't even reach out for my phone, which I'd left there on purpose.

I didn't need any air in my tires, what I had to do was take a moment to think things through. I stretched my arms over my head, enjoyed the pull of my tense muscles as I considered my options. The dangerous bitch was definitely hiding a lot. I'd known from the moment we met, but since then she'd revealed herself to be other. And I couldn't help but remember the vision I'd gotten from her stone—the one still buried deep inside my pocket—about the girl crying black goo.

There was more to her story, and I decided not to kick her out of my car. She'd added the stipulation to ride along with me and was keeping her word by using the stupid rock against me. By forcing me to carry it everywhere to make me a walking, talking beacon.

I sighed, filled my lungs with the fumes of gasoline and oil, and climbed back into Lady Bug to get comfy in the driver's seat.

"Are you feeling better?"

I ignored her and revved the engine.

"Thought you said the tires needed air—"

"I needed air more than they did." Without bothering to look at her, I reversed out of the spot and took a right onto the highway. Most of the traffic headed in the opposite direction, and I was glad.

"I'm really sorry about your face," she whispered.

I kept my eyes on the road and switched the stereo on, smiled as a heavy metal song about exiting the light filled the interior. We were definitely heading into a patch of darkness and it had nothing to do with the lingering dusk threatening to cover the land within the next few hours.

The nun said something else but I couldn't hear her, and that was the way I liked it. I pretended she wasn't there.

Instead, I listened to music and gulped the wind flowing in through the open window. I enjoyed the air buzzing in my ears as my mind wandered all over the landscape. Driving down the highway with a nun in the passenger seat in the hopes of finding an angel somehow matched the metal tunes.

What a strange life you lead. Yet, it was the only one I knew, the one I wanted and deserved.

"Can you turn that down, please?"

"Huh?"

Sister Trinity extended a pale hand, and the crisscrossing scars over the backs stood out under the slant of weak sunlight. She caught my stare and quickly withdrew her hand.

"If you touch my stereo again, I'll add new scars to your collection," I snapped.

"I'm sorry, I didn't mean to offend." Sister Trinity hid both hands in the folds of her armpits and stared ahead.

"Why are you wearing that penguin suit, anyway?" I couldn't bite my tongue any longer. "I thought you lot could wear plain clothes to blend in with everyone else in the twenty-first century."

"They—*we*—can."

"Then why are you heading into the desert wearing clothes that make you look like a penguin?"

She sighed. "It's not a penguin suit. It's called a habit."

"Yeah, a habit, veil, coif, wimple, guimpe, all topped off with a crucifix and rosary," I said, because I'd done my research after meeting her. "I know the names of your fancy dress. I just don't care enough to get it right."

"I understand why you're upset, but that's no excuse to besmirch the Church and—"

"Besmirch the Church?" I snorted. "In case you haven't noticed, I'm a demon, the epitome of what your sanctimonious religion peddles as evil and filth. Yet I'm none of those things. I've spent the majority of my life living amongst humans and have never even come close to killing one." My statement was riddled with lies because I wasn't sure where the people who fell into the pentagram void went, but I had a point to make. "Which is more than I can say for the Catholic Church, which has collected quite the body count throughout history. Way more than Jason, Michael and Freddy combined. With the Inquisition alone, it's enough to rival any tyrant or movie slasher, so don't talk to me about besmirching the fucking Church."

She winced at my words but didn't say anything.

"You haven't answered my question. Why are you wearing a habit like it's the only clothes you have in your closet?" Having a freak in my car repelled me, but I was having too much fun at her expense. And I seemed to be pushing all her buttons, so why hadn't she turned into the other, more violent version of herself yet? What would it take to draw her out?

"I feel more comfortable, closer to God—"

"Bullshit."

Sister Trinity made the sign of the cross and chanted a prayer.

"What's the real reason?" I asked.

"I don't—"

"You do, so answer me."

She wrapped a hand around her rosary and I noticed the small sizzle. Her fingers turned red but she didn't remove them, not even when a wisp of smoke rose from her skin.

I took a deep sniff of the sulfur and almost lost control of the wheel. The discharge from her was pure and unadulterated grade-A brimstone. It wasn't the kind of perfume one would expect from anyone who cried foul on behalf of the Church.

Sister Trinity took her hand off the rosary and closed her eyes, but I'd caught the blink of white. Yet when she opened them, the brown irises were back.

"I feel safer in these clothes." She sighed and considered her burned skin. "Without the habit, veil, and bandeau, I'm not sure how long I will remain myself."

"That's a very cryptic answer, but lucky for you I've already met your alter ego—the Demonic Bitch." I stopped at the red light and turned to glare at her. "That's what she is, right? You're carrying a demon half and she likes to take over. Why isn't she here now? And how did she get into my house?" When dealing with these kinds of people and/or creatures, it was always best to reveal enough information so they knew you were aware of their duality. Leaving some wiggle room also gave them false confidence to assume they held a good dose of ammunition up their sleeves.

"Pretending to be dumber than you are doesn't suit you, *Destiny*." Sister Trinity met my eyes before her gaze strayed to my pocket. "You knew to collect the ash and turn it into an object you're carrying in your pocket."

"Only because Demonic Bitch told me to."

"Can you not call her that?"

"Does she have a proper name? Share it and I'll use it."

A small smile played over her lips. "You're a very clever one, aren't you? She hasn't disclosed her name, but I wouldn't be able to tell you even if I knew."

I shrugged. "It was worth a try."

A beep signaled the light had turned. Why were motorists acting extra pushy on the roads? Didn't people have any patience? I shook my head and continued on but let the impatient vehicle overtake.

"As long as you carry the sulfur, I'll be able to find you wherever you go."

"But that doesn't explain why you weren't physically inside my house."

Trinity sighed and peeked out the side window. "I was outside the house, in the trees behind your cottage. It was as close as I could physically get because of all the protections you've got around your property, but she can astral project inside by using the rock as a beacon. That's how she got in." The nun winced and pressed a hand against her temple. "She doesn't like me sharing her secrets. Almost as much as I don't like the way she uses my body to do less than good deeds."

"This is very interesting. You're telling me that dual citizens live inside you, and that you're the good, she's the bad … who's the ugly?"

"What do you mean?"

I shrugged. "There are three of you in the one body."

"How do you know?"

"Really? You're going to ask me that?" I shook my head. "I can see beyond human and demon. And there's definitely another tucked away inside you."

"I don't want to talk about her," she said. "She rarely makes an appearance."

"Who's the girl, then?"

"What girl?"

"The one with the black tears and the wicked smile."

The sister gasped. "Who told you about her?"

"Your rock gave away a few too many secrets, I think." I shrugged, and stopped at another light. "But it's not the sulfur's fault. I'm very perceptive and can read a lot more than you'd expect."

"What do you mean?"

"Oh, no, I don't share my secrets either. Besides, this isn't about me, it's all about you." Before anyone had the chance to call me out for being too slow, I pressed down on the accelerator when the light turned green. "You're the one who hired us to find an angel. And I'm curious about the girl, that's all."

Tears dribbled down her face but she didn't wipe them away.

I handed her a tissue.

"Thank you." Trinity dabbed her cheeks.

Damn this temperamental woman. Looked like the little girl could be another trigger. For the sake of solving the case and because we still had quite a bit of road to travel before we reached our destination, I decided to focus on what really mattered.

"Tell me more about the angel."

The ringtone on my phone filled the car before she could answer. I didn't need to check because I recognized Kenan's ringtone, but she snuck a look.

When the ringing stopped, she said, "Erela is a Cherubim, a Guardian of Children and the Innocent. The one who watches over all who are pure."

"Well, she fails to protect them, doesn't she?" I shook my head, but at least her answer matched what I already knew, and what she'd told us. "And many times, from the clergy. I wonder how a guardian feels about that fact?"

The ringtone cut through our conversation, and I ignored it again.

"It's true." Sister Trinity twisted the tissue around her fingers. "The very men who are supposed to provide comfort and safety let the rest of us down."

"Maybe the Catholic Church should allow their priests to enjoy the wonderful pleasures of consensual sex between *consenting adults* like the rest of us." I probably came across like a flippant asshole to her, but it made sense to me. Why deprive people from sexual pleasure at the expense of abuse masked by claims of celibacy?

"You might think it's strange, but I agree with you. The Church needs to admit that the men of the cloth are flesh and blood and have the same urges as everyone else."

"I think that should extend to nuns too. I mean, seriously, isn't it enough punishment that you can't even become priests?"

She surprised me with a laugh. "You have a very crude way of wording things, but you're right. Still, one person can't change the world."

"No, but a movement can. Maybe you need to talk to your fellow penguin girls and bring forth the tide of change."

"I've got my own problems without adding anything that big to the list."

"Anyway, let's get back to the angel," I said.

My mobile rang and I rolled my eyes, tightened my grip on the wheel.

"Yes, Erela." Sister Trinity glanced at the glowing screen. "She serves the highest seat in the Cherubim order so she watches over the children and manages the angels in her care. She's very important, and for her to be lost, it means there are a great many disruptions happening above. Having no leader must have sent everyone into a frenzy both above and below."

"Okay, see, that's where you lose me." I shook my head. "I get that she's a big deal and all of that, but how do you keep up with what's going on *up there*? Especially since you're not even attached to an actual parish."

"Excuse me?"

My bombshell had the desired effect and it made me smile.

"You didn't think we would do a background check? Wow, that's a bit arrogant, wouldn't you say? Zenda Sagar is a thorough investigator and she called around to all the local churches. Yet, no one claimed you. No one knows who you are, Sister Trinity."

She tore the tissue to bits on her lap but didn't say anything.

My phone to rang another two times between my accusation and her silence.

"You better not get any of those scraps on the floor of Lady Bug."

"Who's Lady Bug?"

I rolled my eyes. "My car, of course."

"You named your car?"

"Doesn't everyone?"

"I've never had one."

"Anyway, back to the angel and the rogue nun."

"Okay, you've got me," Trinity said. "I'm not actually employed or on active duty with any parish at the moment. I did have a teaching position at Saint Clara's Immaculate Rose Catholic Church until a few years ago."

"Oh yeah, what happened? You got tired of measuring all of those skirt uniform hems and wanted more of a challenge?" I laughed at my own joke and hit the steering wheel for effect. The religious jokes wrote themselves.

"*No*, I set out on a personal quest no one wanted to help me with."

"What's that?"

"Helping a possessed child that the Church refused to exorcise." She licked her lips. "That's why I took things into my own hands—"

"And ended up possessed yourself." I cut her off. My vision finally made total sense.

Sister Trinity sighed.

"Don't be upset or surprised, I get the picture. You were trying to help a possessed girl and inadvertently welcomed the demon into your body. It's a very noble risk to take. No wonder you ended up with the baggage instead." I didn't add what a severe risk such a decision posed to the unqualified.

Demons were tricksters and although a lot were impassive, exceptions to the rule always had to be taken into consideration. The reputation of evil came from somewhere.

"Why didn't the Church help you afterwards?" I asked.

"I didn't tell them."

"Why not?"

"It's … complicated."

"Demonic possession usually is, but that's no reason to turn their back on you when you needed them the most." I didn't understand people. "They probably would've helped if you'd asked, right?"

"Let's just say I've burned too many bridges with the Church," she said. "I'm on my own."

"If you're not associated with the Church, how did you find out about Erela?"

"I still have associates and contacts who keep me in the loop. And when I heard about what happened, I wanted to search for her before anyone else."

"Will the Church send out their own crew as well?" I didn't like the idea of competition on this quest. My personal stake in this situation seemed to grow by the minute. Not only was I linked to Erela, but I had the inside scoop on the woman who started everything. The rogue nun carrying two passengers within her body had an interesting story to tell. I hadn't expected her problems to stem from a botched exorcism.

I couldn't wait to talk to Zenda.

"I honestly don't think they'll bother." Trinity snorted. "Several days had already passed when I found out and they hadn't done anything. The Church likes to talk about Heaven as if it's an extension of themselves but rarely bother to engage. They don't even want to deal with demonic threats anymore. Do you have any idea how many times priests have been sent out to assess a situation only to pin it on mental health? It's why I took matters into my own hands and tried to save the girl. I couldn't let them walk away and allow that demon to corrupt and compel her to infect others." Tears dripped down her face and I handed her another tissue. "I just couldn't."

My mobile rang.

Damn it, Kenan. Not now!

I waited a few beats before speaking. "We're probably on our own in the search for Erela, and I prefer it that way. Like I told you back at the office—I like to work alone. You decided to ignore what I said and invited yourself along for the ride, but I can't pretend what you're telling me isn't helpful. What I don't understand is why you didn't provide all of the details at the beginning." I snuck a quick peek at her but she was watching the road. "It would've saved a lot of discomfort and suspicion."

"I'd intended to come clean when we were well on our way." She glanced at me quickly. "I gather patience isn't one of your virtues, which isn't surprising considering your nature."

"Oh yeah? What nature is that?"

Sister Trinity's gaze snapped back toward me, and she checked out my horns. "You're a demon, of course."

"You're very perceptive." I stopped at what I knew would be the last set of lights before the highway morphed into a freeway. "And quite sneaky."

Traffic had thinned out and we were alone, so no one beeped.

"I'm not either of those things. If I was, you wouldn't have figured out this much about my situation," she said.

Kenan's ring tone cut into the silence.

"Aren't you going to answer that?"

"Nope."

Trinity eyed the mobile. "This Kenan person really wants to get in touch with you. Maybe it's an emergency."

"It's not." Another lie because I considered any and all interactions with him to be emergencies. As much as I itched to pick up, I couldn't bring myself to answer with an audience.

"If you say so."

"I say so."

"You're very prickly, aren't you?"

I flashed her a glare. "Is that a dig at my horns?"

"No."

"You can see them, right?" My glamour was active, and walking around the gas station earlier had confirmed the fact because no one stopped to stare or made outraged comments. Yet it wasn't surprising that Trinity—touched by the demonic—could see them.

"They're a bit hazy at the moment," she answered. "Why is that?"

"Because I don't want to scare everyone. Besides, unlike some people, I prefer to blend into a crowd." Not to mention stay under the radar of those who might hunt me down. Supernatural TV shows had taught me that Zenda and Mer were right—*it's important to keep my head down.* Or in my case, horns and hooves.

"That's true," she said with a smile. "The last thing you want to do is start a panic. Or get the attention of the Church. *That* would ensure they started paying attention. The downside would be the same unfortunate thing that happened the last time they claimed demons walked the Earth."

"Oh yeah, what's that?"

"The Inquisition."

After her sobering answer, we settled into a few minutes of blissful silence and I let the wind blowing in through the window raise the hair off the back of my neck. Strands flew into my face and the rest got tangled around my horns.

At least Sister Trinity's presence hadn't stolen the carefree feeling I associated with road trips. I hated to admit it, but she was better company than I'd expected. She'd provided very helpful info and wasn't entirely awful. Aside from her creepy half, who enjoyed traipsing through my house, spying and judging, I could get used to having her around. Maybe she'd become a contact worth keeping.

Also, realizing the Church was careless, lazy, and didn't care about the interference of angels and demons in this world made my job easier—*better.*

No wonder Trinity was the only clergy from whom we'd received any kind of pushback. It also explained why they often hired Zenda instead of tackling such issues internally. If only the Church was open about other facets of their organization. Maybe then fewer kids would fall prey to the predators shrouded within.

It reminded me of something else.

"You know, it seems to me like those guardian angels aren't doing enough to protect children. Doesn't that bother you?" I said, glancing at her. I often wondered why it didn't bother the priests. Many had to be decent men. "Too many kids get hurt all over the world and they're not—"

"Look out!"

I turned in time to see the oncoming bus.

The large vehicle skidded all over the road and headed straight for us, but it wasn't corporeal. I slammed on the brakes and Lady Bug squealed to a stop as the bus collided with the front bumper, but didn't crunch or send us spinning out of control.

Instead, we were suddenly *inside*, watching the driver and passengers scream as they held on, eyes fixed on the windows with horror. The piercing cries and the terror in their dead orbs haunted me, but no one reacted to our presence.

Spirits trapped inside their tomb.

"Holy shit." I'd never seen anything like it before.

I inhaled ice particles that crystalized in my lungs. The assault induced a coughing fit, which the nun echoed. Cold conditions played havoc on our demonic bodies and I couldn't catch my breath to fight against suffocation. I clutched my chest, hoping it would clear the painful chill.

The sensation seemed to go on forever but only lasted as long as it took the length of the bus to get through and past us. Once the large vehicle cleared the car, we both somehow found the energy to turn and look out the back window and watch the bus drive into a ditch. It landed on its side and I could hear the shrieking before a ball of fire erupted, leaving behind an unnatural silence.

"What on earth … just happened?" the nun panted.

I caught my breath. "Spirit bus."

"I didn't know such a thing existed." Her eyes were as wide as saucers.

"You've never seen a ghost?"

"I've seen plenty of ghosts, but always tied to a house or a place of some sort."

"This particular one is tied to this freeway." I considered her while trying to collect my thoughts and calm my pulse. "Surely you've heard the stories about phantom hitchhikers and girls who appear in your backseat only to vanish when you've reached their destination?"

"I have," she said. "But I thought they were urban legends, myths people like to tell each other to scare wary travelers."

"Some might be, but all folklore comes from a true source." I smiled, which did nothing to ease the pain in my chest. "One great entity creating the world and the cosmos only to let it turn to shit is the biggest story of them all. Isn't it?"

"God isn't an urban legend or folklore—"

"But he's part of mythology," I interrupted. "Which is actually my point. How can you believe in one God and not suspect ghosts are everywhere?"

"You don't believe in God?"

"No."

"What about the Devil?"

"I don't believe in him either."

She frowned. "How do you explain who you are, then?"

The fact she said *who* rather than *what* somewhat endeared her to me even more.

"Hey, I didn't say I don't believe in Heaven and Hell, angels and demons, I said I don't believe in God and the Devil. They're obviously fabrications meant to personify good and evil. A convenient way to fool and control humans." I'd spent many hours pondering that particular line of logic. "I believe in the hierarchies of both places and think there are leaders who rule their respective legions and choirs."

"You believe Heaven and Hell are more like Greek mythology?" Sister Trinity seemed intrigued by that notion, which made me like her even more. If we weren't careful, we might spend hours discussing the countless possibilities.

"In a way."

"I find the concept fascinating …" Trinity was quiet for a moment, thoughtful. "You see them like Mount Olympus and Hades."

"It makes sense, right?"

She didn't say anything for a while. "Yes, I can see what you're saying."

"Good to see we agree on something!"

"It's sad, though." Her eyes glistened with unshed tears. "Is there anything we can do to help?"

"Help who?"

"The bus."

"No, they're caught in a loop on this stretch of road and won't ever stop."

"Ever?"

I shrugged. "Well, until someone is able to help them crossover, I suppose."

"Can't you do that?"

"I'm a demon, not a bloody spook catcher or psychopomp!"

The sister appeared much smaller, almost timid. "I wish we could help them …"

"So do I. But the best thing we can do is to keep going before it comes around again." I'd always considered myself lucky to have avoided such a phenomenon. Now that I had, I didn't want to feel its chilling effects a second time.

"The world is such a strange place." Her voice softened, yet seemed huskier.

I turned to face her and the white pieces of her outfit glowed. Scars crisscrossed her face and her eyes were a transparent creamy color.

What the hell is going on?

Sister Trinity's serene smile made the lingering chill effects slide away. I decided not to bother asking any questions, having a feeling the third passenger sharing her body had dropped in.

I straightened in my seat and was about to restart Lady Bug when she placed a gentle hand on my forearm.

"Wait," she said.

"For what?"

"Until the bus returns."

"There's no way I'm going to go through that—"

"Please," the nun said and those uncanny eyes filled me with comfortable warmth, a cocoon of cozy comfort I didn't want to escape.

I knew that no matter what, she'd keep me safe. "Let's wait, it won't take long."

I nodded absently, turned away, and pressed the back of my head against the headrest because the world had taken on a much lighter and sharper glow. Somewhere in the distance, my phone rang, but I couldn't move.

"Here they are."

"Who?"

"The unfortunate souls." Sister Trinity left the VW and stepped into the middle of the road, in front of the approaching bus. She raised both arms before her and her skin lit up so bright my eyes teared up, but I didn't look away. I saw her reach for the passengers and catch their attention.

The nun is stronger than the loop they're trapped in.

The bus drove through her and Sister Trinity attracted every single person to her like a magnet. All the spirits stuck inside the doomed vehicle transformed into tiny specks of golden light and she blew each one into the darkening sky.

By the time the bus reached Lady Bug, it was empty and faded. I closed my eyes anyway because it stung my corneas. Even behind my eyelids, I could still see the wonder. The magic the nun had performed imprinted into my vision. She had too many fucking secrets.

"Are you ready to go?"

My eyes snapped open and I found her sitting in the passenger seat as if she'd never left my side. Her familiar brown eyes had replaced the spooky ones and her scarred hands rested in her lap. Yet I knew what I'd seen. She'd accomplished a feat only a ghost hunter or psychopomp could complete. Who *was* the third entity she carried around with her?

"What are you?" I whispered.

"I'm Sister Trinity, a nun who needs you to get going. We've already wasted a lot of valuable time." Her eyes sparkled. "We've got an angel to find and the clock is ticking."

I shook my head in wonder and started the engine before driving off, leaving the miracle in my rearview mirror.

Chapter Twelve

"Are you sure we have to stop?"

"I'm positive," I said for what had to be the tenth time. The nun had asked the same question when I'd parked, as we walked to the office while we waited for the clerk, during the booking, and as soon as we went outside with keys in hand. "My back is sore and I need some sleep. Besides, we're not driving out into the middle of nowhere in the dark."

Plus, I need to sort through that shit you did out there in the middle of the freeway.

We didn't talk about what happened and drove the last few hours without a single word. I couldn't stop thinking about that bizarre experience. How could a rogue nun carrying a demonic parasite manage to perform a holier than thou deed? A miracle of sorts. She was definitely a conundrum, a puzzle I needed to solve during our adventure.

"I offered to drive, but you kept saying no."

"No one drives Lady Bug but me!"

"Okay, okay."

"This is yours." I handed her the key with the room number seven printed on the white plastic fob. "We've got the rooms until tomorrow morning and we're next to each other. In case there's an *emergency*." Had to make sure she understood that I needed a break from her. "Only if it's a real emergency, okay? I need my beauty sleep and have plenty of work to do. After all, this isn't a vacation."

"Is there anything I can do to help?"

"No, I can handle it." The thought of spending another minute with the freaky chick made my skin itch. A few more hours weren't going to make much of a difference to the angel who didn't know I was on my way to—hopefully—rescue her.

At least, that's what I kept telling myself, which was hard to do when Erela's plea for help and those weird visions of feathers and blood still plagued me.

Horned Lady, if you can hear me, please find me before I lose myself completely.

Yeah, I'm on my way.

Several concerns troubled me while in the middle of nowhere. The main one I couldn't shake was what Sister Trinity had done on the freeway. How had she been able to release those spirits from their endless cycle? How could a freak who'd hurt me back at the house make me feel relaxed and safe? The experience screwed with my expectations of the woman, and I hadn't bothered asking any questions. About anything.

"Has anyone ever told you your face turns to stone, like a statue, when you're caught up in your thoughts?"

I shook everything away but her annoying comment. "Yes, I'm well aware and don't need you to remind me about my freaky ways."

"I didn't say you were freaky, just strange."

"Same thing." My fingers went to my face "At least the scratch you gave me is gone."

She lowered her gaze. "I'm sorry."

I sighed, because how could I accept an apology from the part of her who hadn't actually hurt me? My life was getting weirder by the minute.

"Well, I guess I should get some rest." Sister Trinity yawned and considered the key before heading for the blue door labeled with a plastic number seven. I'd taken six. By mistake, yet very symbolic. "Guess I'll see you tomorrow."

"You better set your alarm because we're heading out at five."

She nodded. "I'll be ready."

"Good."

Sister Trinity waved and stopped in front of the dirty door, but peeked over her shoulder. "You can ask me the question you've been meaning to ask since it happened. I don't mind."

"Oh, all of a sudden you're willing to talk about it."

A rueful smile teased her pretty face. "Suppose I deserve that, but some things are easier said than others."

"I get it. You mean, you're more than happy to share the braggy stuff but not very forward about the much darker things," I said with a lighter tone than I'd intended.

"I don't brag. The Demonic Bitch might like to, but the rest of us don't."

I returned the smile because I appreciated the olive branch. "How you created that spirit lightshow isn't as important as the fact you did it. Because of you, those lost souls were able to move on. Instead of being stuck in a ghoulish cycle that's guaranteed to scare the shit out of anyone unfortunate enough to witness the display." Me, included.

"That's what I hope we can do when we reach Erela."

"Why do I feel like you're leaving out some very important details about that?"

She shrugged. "You'll see everything for yourself soon."

"I'm sure I will."

"Well, good night." As she headed inside, a second before the door closed, she called, "I'm glad you've finally met all of us."

I stood in the dark parking lot for several quiet minutes, watching her room. I wanted to make sure she stayed inside. Funny how someone could be many things at once. The trick Trinity performed on the freeway was the stuff of miracles. Daytime movie kind of magic that didn't fit into the world I'd learned to accept as my own.

There are more things in heaven and earth. Not to mention in hell…

The only light over my head flickered before fizzling out completely, only to come back to life. I didn't like the strange vibrations in the air. Shadows accumulated on the other side of the road, accompanied by childish giggles and small footsteps.

Surely no one brought their kids to such a sad motel?

I sighed and while considering my own key the phone tucked into my back pocket started ringing. I'd avoided Kenan for too long. The fact he kept calling and refused to leave a message or send a text worried and irritated me. Why did he want to drive me crazy with endless calls?

Should've turned my phone off.

I ignored the prickling sensation of being watched and strolled to the door, unlocked it, and stepped inside my room. Headlights lit up the window after I closed myself in for the night, a bright splash of dazzling illumination the flimsy curtains couldn't shroud.

Looks like we're not the only desperados around here tonight.

My mobile rang again and this time I answered. "Hey, Kenan."

"Hey, Kenan?" He sighed. *"That's all you've got to say? I've been calling you for hours and when you finally decide to answer, that's all you can think to say?"* He didn't seem angry, more panicked than anything else.

"You know I don't have hands-free in Lady Bug. I can't answer the phone while I'm driving." Did he call to annoy me? "Besides, I texted you before. You could've responded to that."

"No, I couldn't." Kenan sounded like he was getting out of his car, crunching over the gravel as he spoke. "I need to speak to you in person."

"Yeah, well, maybe I'm not ready to speak to—"

"Des, what I said earlier was pathetic and wrong—"

"You were fucking out of line," I cut him off. "Not to mention rude. What possessed you to say those things in front of Zenda? Say whatever you want to me, but she didn't deserve that disrespect."

His hurried breath carried through the phoneline. "Neither of you deserved what I did. I'm sorry. I really am. I lost my mind and ..."

"Look, I'm in the middle of this case and need to figure a few things out before I head out tomorrow. We'll talk when I get home."

"How about we talk now?"

"I thought you wanted to speak to me in person and I'm kilometers away."

The knock on the door made my heart stutter. Was the nun getting antsy already? Well, I wasn't going to supply support or entertainment.

"Kenan, I have to go, there's someone at the door."

"Yes, there is."

"What? How could you know?" What the hell was going on with him? One second, he wanted to talk in person. The next, he knew about the knocking on my motel room. I made my way to the door and when I pulled it open, there he was. Kenan, with a backpack hanging off one shoulder, more disheveled than he'd been before and still holding the phone to his ear. "What are you doing here?"

"I couldn't leave things that way ..."

Hearing his answer in my ear and in front of me unnerved me so I disconnected and lowered the phone to my side. "But how did you get here?"

"I drove." He hitched a thumb over his shoulder to his parked car, in the spot next to Lady Bug. "I wanted to catch up with you sooner but Zenda insisted I listen to everything she had to say first." He sighed. "I knew where you were going and—"

"You followed me! You haven't got a tracker on my phone, have you?" The thought of him keeping tabs on me made me uncomfortable. I wanted to be with him, but I didn't like the idea of surveilling each other. "Or in my car?"

"Auntie does. She's got it on both of our phones to make sure we're safe."

"Yeah, Zenda has an app on her laptop because it's her company policy. But it doesn't explain how you have access."

"I'd prefer not to answer that." Kenan disconnected and pocketed his mobile. "Besides, I saw Lady Bug in the parking lot as I drove past. I wasn't tracking you. Not exactly."

"Ah, how convenient."

"Can I come in?"

I left him hanging for several beats. I wouldn't deny him entry but wanted to make him sweat a little. It was the least he deserved after everything he'd said and done. But this was Kenan, standing outside my motel room. He'd cared enough to chase after me.

To some, it might seem a bit much and raise red flags of the stalkerish kind, but Kenan wasn't like that. He wanted to make amends. His earlier behavior had thrown me for a loop, but after everything, I still felt the same way about him. I'd sent him a text to tell him exactly how I felt, so he had to know that in spite of his irrational reaction, I loved him.

I opened the door wider and he stepped inside.

"Des, I'm very sorry."

"I am too." I locked the door because we didn't need any interruptions.

"It's just ..." He ran a hand through his hair, making it stick up. "Not going with you after everything ... I lost control, and couldn't stop my confusion from turning into rage."

"Now you understand how I feel." I sympathized with that much, especially after reading Zenda's text message. "You always wondered about how fast my rage rose to the surface. Well, congrats! You have firsthand experience."

"It's not a good feeling." He stood in front of the door, uncertain. Keeping his distance and avoiding my eyes. "I'm sorry."

"Why did you come all this way?"

Kenan made eye contact and licked his lips.

"Well?"

"I had to come because I've found out some things I have to tell you."

"Oh yeah, like what?"

"Like ..." His voice trailed off as he took off his glasses, shoved them into his backpack and kicked his shoes off. He took a single step. "Important things you need to hear."

"Tell me, what's it about?"

He dropped the bag and closed the distance. One more tiny step would bring us together.

"It's uh …"

Like two magnets unable to control themselves, we were suddenly pressed against each other. Our lips glued together in a passionate kiss, while his hands ran over my back and my fingers got lost in his messy hair.

"We shouldn't be doing this," I said, pulling away. "There's a lot to do and even more to sort through."

"Yes, there is." Yet, his mouth returned to mine, his tongue slipped inside and his hands cupped my butt. I wrapped my legs around his hips.

"We should really stop and leave this for later," I whispered against his lips before returning for more.

"I agree."

Kenan carried me to the bed, threw me on the lumpy mattress and landed on top of me. We tore the clothes off each other until there was nothing to separate our bodies. His skin felt hot against mine and when he nudged my legs apart and entered me, I cried out in pure ecstasy.

I raked my nails over his back and he closed his eyes for a second.

"You drive me wild," he whispered.

"I know."

Kenan met my eyes and lowered his chest against my breasts as he took my hands and raised them above my head. He laced his fingers around mine and pushed inside me in a slow pace that drove me crazy. I tilted my hips to receive him, intensifying the angle to meet every thrust and ensure he rubbed me up the right way.

"Faster," I said.

Kenan picked up the pace and when the hectic rhythm pushed us over the edge, we both cried out at the same time.

Our breaths became the only noise inside the room.

"I'm sorry that was … fast," he said in my ear.

"Quickies are as good as marathons." I wasn't going to complain, not after such an explosive reunion. I hadn't expected to have sex inside a shitty motel room with the man who'd been so angry with me he'd walked out of my house. I'd planned on a lonely night to think, sort, and probably avoid his calls. Considering everything that happened, his surprise turned out to be a much better way to start the evening.

"Well,"—he skimmed his lips over my skin, in a very suggestive way—"I'm not done with you yet."

"But we have heaps to do and even more to talk about—"

"Oh, we'll be doing a lot of talking. Or at least, our bodies will." Kenan stood and offered me a hand. When I took it, he led me into the small bathroom with the chipped tiles and the cramped shower for round two of what I hoped led to a lot more.

CHAPTER THIRTEEN

"I can't believe you drove for hours to make a booty call," I teased, ruffling Kenan's damp hair away from his handsome face. We were stretched out in bed, naked and feeling fresh after a nice, long shower.

He'd hauled a selection of junk food and drinks from the vending machine outside our room and dumped everything on the bed. The sugary and salty packs weren't ideal food picks because Zenda had instilled good eating habits in both of us, but they provided nourishment for tonight.

Besides, highly processed foods didn't have a negative effect on me.

"Des, that's not what I did."

"Yeah, well, tell that to my throbbing loins." I laughed at his appalled reaction. All the tension and anger he'd projected back home had subsided completely. The power of sex could ease just about any ailment.

Most human and demons knew about the many benefits. It was why demoniacs preferred to use sex when making power plays and deals. After blissful, pleasurable encounters humans were a lot more manageable, like supple taffy willing to be twisted and contorted.

A lot of deals and many souls had been signed away during the effects of afterglow. I knew because I'd had to deal with my fair share of cases that involved cleaning up the aftereffects of these chaotic unions.

That wasn't what I was doing with Kenan, but the reality of how I affected him during and after intimacy intrigued me. I'd actually noticed his increased strength and how well he coped with positions in cramped areas. He was also faster, could withstand more, and his eyes shone red when he came.

Another tiny tidbit I wouldn't tell him. Not yet. Maybe he'd discover the abilities for himself, but for the moment my wicked little secrets would stay with me.

I couldn't pretend I didn't like the physical stamina, but worried about the long-term effects of his entanglement with me. Would I change him completely? Would I encroach on his lifespan in a positive or negative way? Zenda mentioned I had a positive effect on her mortality, but she'd been altered before I came along. Kenan was different. He was all human.

I had to find out more.

"You're a wicked woman."

His accusation roused me back from my thoughts. "Says the man who drove all afternoon to barge into my motel room to seduce poor, unsuspecting me." I batted my eyelashes and cracked up. "You're too easy to bait."

"And you're very wicked."

"You already said that."

"Seriously, though." Kenan leaned back against the headboard and distracted me with his firm chest and the light sprinkling of hair. "I'm glad we sorted things out because I can't be far from you for long. It drives me crazy. It's always been that way. I hated going back to boarding school because I couldn't stand to be away after summer was over. That's why I prefer university. It keeps me closer to you." He took my hand and laced his fingers around mine and his gray eyes looked vibrant without his glasses. "What I'm trying to say is …" He sighed. "Listen, when I got your text, I wanted to respond but it didn't feel right. I had to tell you in person."

"Kenan, what are you trying to say?" The suspense was killing me.

"I feel the same way." He met my gaze and I could read the intensity and honesty. "I've been in love with you for so long it started to hurt right here." Kenan pressed our joined hands against his chest, over his beating heart. "Destiny, I love you."

"I love you too, Kenan." I smiled. "A text wasn't the best way to tell you, but you were angry and I needed you to understand that I wasn't upset. I might've been pissed off enough to walk out on you back at Zenda's, but I can't stay angry with you."

"I need you to hold onto that thought when I confess the rest."

I sat up and our hands slid away from each other. "What is it?"

He turned away, focused on the shabby wall instead of my breasts.

I clutched his chin and forced him to look at me. "Kenan, spit it out. Tell me already."

"I have a lot of things to tell you, it's another reason why I rushed over," he said. "But this might upset you and I don't want us to—"

"Just tell me. What's going on?" I wasn't sure what to expect, but his reaction concerned me.

"I found out how to get back to Hell," Kenan blurted. "I've known for several months."

"What?"

"I figured out how demons can get back to Hell a few months ago."

"Why didn't you tell me?"

Kenan ran a hand through his damp hair. "Because finding out how it can be done isn't the same as actually telling you how to get there."

"I have no clue what that means." Why would he keep something that important from me? Was it a selfish way to keep me with him, on this realm? Was it because he wanted to find out every minute detail before telling me? I had every right to be upset about his omission, but I couldn't grasp a single one. I'd done the same to Zenda when it came to the nun's ashy discharge.

As much as his revelation shocked me, I refused to get angry. I decided to let him spill everything—including his reasons for leaving me out of the pact we'd made.

"It means that you need to find an access point," he said. "It's called a Hellmouth. It's also the only way a demon can get back into Hell."

"That's it? We need to find a portal that I can go through?" Nothing in life was ever that easy. Especially when it came to the demonic.

"Well, that's the problem. A Hellmouth is found in very specific places around the globe and I've been trying to locate the closest one. They're a combination of ley line intersections and hidden magical spots." He licked his lips. The scholar side of Kenan was hard to silence when he got rolling. "Although it's taken me ages to figure out, this afternoon I finally worked out where one is located."

"Where?"

"There's one near the shed where you found Rosie."

"*What?*"

"There's a Hellmouth somewhere near the shed," he repeated with a curt nod. "That's what I think the word Hell meant in reference to your mind-soar. And I don't think it's a coincidence that it's close to where Erela is imprisoned."

"You're right, it can't be a coincidence." Could this be why that particular spot had turned up in my mind-soar twice already? At the time, I hadn't understood the reason. I remembered when I'd searched for Rosie, and how even after finding her discarded body inside the shed, the sense of being watched had been strong. But not as powerful as the strange and familiar sensation prickling over my skin. I'd ignored both impressions and assumed the effect to be nothing more than extrasensory sensitivity. But, in light of what Kenan had just told me, it could only mean one thing. "A demonic must have Erela."

"It's possible."

"Okay. I find this Hellmouth, walk through and that's it?" Better to concentrate on the positive than the confusing.

Kenan shook his head. "It's more complicated than that because you also need the location of your legion."

"I don't know anything about any legion." There went that idea. "I don't remember where I came from or who summoned me. Guess we're back to square one." I sat back and a thought struck me. A worm of an idea that could be nothing or everything. "Wait a second! What happens if I go through anyway?"

"Well, if you cross into Hell without a precise position in mind or without an allegiance to any particular legion, you could end up anywhere or nowhere. Might get lost forever. It's why I wanted to wait before telling you." Kenan regarded me, probably trying to gauge my reaction. "But when I found out there was a Hellmouth where you were headed, I had to tell you."

I cupped his face and kissed his nose. "It's okay, I'm not angry with you."

"Really?"

"Really."

"Are you sure?"

I smiled, nodded. "I'm fine, but I keep waiting for the punchline."

"Ah, you know me too well." He squeezed my hand, could barely contain his excitement. "I worked out where you were born. As well as the legion you belong to."

I sat up straighter, and his hand slid away again. "How is that possible?"

"The book I showed you at your house led me to other texts and I fell down a demonic rabbit hole," he said. "So, I went to the archival occult section at the library and figured out a lot of very interesting things."

"Well, don't keep me in suspense."

"The sigil on your horn belongs to a demon president called, Foras."

"Foras?" I tested the name to see if it sparked a memory, or would somehow unlock hidden secrets trapped inside my head, but I had nothing. I was still as confused as I'd been a minute earlier. "The name doesn't mean anything to me."

"President Foras commands twenty-nine legions," Kenan said, and he became a lecturer rather than a student. "He teaches arts, logic and ethics as well as the virtues of herbs and precious stones. He can also make man eloquent or invisible and bestow longer life. He can recover treasures …"

"What are you leaving out?"

"Foras manifests as a tall, muscly man with horns and he can find lost things."

"That's what I can do! I find lost things." I reached for my horns but stopped midway. "Does that mean *I'm* this president guy?"

I studied my feminine attributes and wondered if demonic texts got the gender wrong. From what I read, every demon was always referred to as male, but surely that couldn't be right. There had to be plenty of female demoniacs with legions to rule over.

"No, you're not him. But you *are* part of his legion."

"Okay."

"Do you remember the charms that were hooked around your horns when you came through? We thought the one and the three might be your age, didn't we?"

I nodded because without any real evidence, we'd based my current age on those charms.

"I think the numbers are supposed to be thirty-one, not thirteen." He pointed at a page in the book. "Thirty-one is his place in the Lesser Key of Solomon."

"But who am I, then?"

"The sigil on your horn confirms that you're not him because a President of Hell wouldn't be branded. They mark their kindred with their sigil," Kenan said. "I think the conjurer wanted to summon Foras, but got you instead."

That made sense. I arrived and was such a disappointment the summoner abandoned me.

"I'm sorry, Des."

"What a terrible thing to do …" I swallowed the pain.

"It's cruel and unfair."

I didn't respond. Couldn't. Fury coiled inside my stomach when I recalled the confusion I felt as soon as I'd opened my eyes and found myself in a strange land without a single memory. Nothing to help me figure out who I was, where I'd come from, or what I was doing in a dirty alley. The only answer I got was the chalk and bloody pentagram on the brick wall behind me, to confirm I'd been summoned.

My tail and cloven hooves indicated I was a dark creature, some sort of freak. It took a long while to muster both the strength and courage to leave that dingy and dark place. If it hadn't been for the drunken, laughing voices that hurt my sensitive senses, I never would've ventured out onto the street in the dead of night. I wouldn't have ended up in Zenda's backyard with a cramped stomach, determined to go through her trash in hopes of finding a scrap to eat.

"Holy shit! Des, you have to calm down."

If not for Zenda's love and attention, I probably would have died on the streets. She'd been very kind and had no qualms about inviting me into her exciting and strange life. That woman had never showed an ounce of fear and her patience helped me accept my fate. Because of her, I chose to live.

"Des, the abyss is getting bigger!"

"Huh?" I blinked and focused on his face and beard, on what he was trying to tell me. Kenan's eyes were wide and terrified, small flames reflected in his irises.

When I followed his gaze, I found the fiery pentagram void glowing bright as the black hole near the end of the bed expanded. The threadbare rug the motel owners used to hide the stained and worn carpet had burned to dust, or got lost in the obscurity. One foot of the bed's frame was already sinking in.

"Shit!" I sucked in a deep breath and sighed, released the anger until my vision returned to normal.

The hole vanished but I could taste sulfur on my lips.

"That was close," Kenan said with a whistle. "Are you okay?"

"Yeah. Sorry, I got sucked into some really bad memories."

"Don't be sorry." He ran his fingers over my face and wiped away the tears. "I understand what it's like to feel abandoned."

I hated to remind him about the loss of his parents. When it happened, Kenan's grief had often manifested in bouts of anger. Always aimed at his parents.

"I can't believe I'm a minion, like those pathetic yellow things everyone hates." I had to change the subject. "What possessed me to think—even for a second—that *I* could actually be important? I'm just another pathetic demon."

"Hey, you're not pathetic and you *are* important. You matter to me and Zenda, to Mer and her pack—you are worth everything to us." Kenan knelt in front of me. "Besides, that's not what a minion is." He shook his head and chuckled. "You're the minion of a President of Hell who can find things. It totally fits. How many times have you wondered why it's easy for you to mind-soar and locate missing people? This is why!"

I smiled at him because Kenan meant the world to me. *I'm so lucky to have him in my life.*

"Thank you," I said.

"No need to thank me."

I took a deep breath and exhaled. "How do I get back?" The question to end all questions. The reason why we'd kept our stupid crusade a secret from Zenda.

After confessing our love for each other and consummating the passion we'd ignored for years, I didn't want to go anywhere. Not because it turned out that I wasn't important—even if the word minion made me feel like a useless worker ant—but because we deserved a chance at happiness. In the human world I had family, friends, people I cared about.

What if no one was waiting on the other side? Or worse, what if the president who owned me found out I was back? Minions probably didn't have parents. No brothers or sisters. In the underworld I'd be one of many, part of a huge clan. One insignificant nobody who'd been in the wrong place at the wrong time and ended up taking the place of her boss.

"Hey, are you still with me?" Kenan caressed my face.

At least I hadn't tried to destroy the motel room during my latest mind-slip.

"Yeah, I'm here, just thinking about how insubstantial I—"

"I've already told you, but I'll tell you again. You're not insubstantial to me," he said, rubbing a thumb over my lips. "Or to Auntie Zenda or Mer. Not to all the people you've helped along the way. Or the ones who weren't quite people and needed the kind of assistance no one else would've been able to provide. You matter to us. And especially to me."

I sighed. "I'm sorry. Just having a bit of a pity party because reality is nothing like fiction." Funny thing was, I hadn't had any dreams of grandeur, but being one of many and easily forgotten had hit harder than I'd expected.

"No, reality can be even better than fiction." Kenan leaned over and kissed me.

"Okay, how do we do this?" I asked. We'd wasted too much time and energy to give up now.

"We find the Hellmouth and you step through." He didn't take his off mine. "The sigil on your horn will do the rest."

"It's that easy?" I still wasn't convinced.

"Well, it's that easy to pass the threshold and get to wherever it is you were born," Kenan said. "But after that, you could end up anywhere."

"Imagine if I arrive and the official who organizes the demons who've been away from Hell puts me in quarantine. Or in jail? What if returning without permission is frowned upon?" My mind raced. "I've crossed paths with a lot of people possessed by demons and the demonic's main concern is always about going back. There's got to be a reason. They must fear returning to their rightful place a lot more than the thought of stealing a human body. It's insane to think about."

"Are you having second thoughts?"

"I'm having second and third thoughts." What he'd uncovered changed everything. Was curiosity about my origins worth losing everything and everyone? Why bother going to an unknown place when I had a comfortable life? It wasn't worth risking my loving family and friends, a fantastic job I enjoyed and was good at. What would be the point of destroying everything I valued?

Is finding out where you came from really worth all this trouble?

Maybe losing my memory had been a blessing in disguise.

"Whatever you decide, I'll support you." Kenan held my hands between his and squeezed.

"You have no idea how much that means to me." I loved him more than anything, and had for ages. How could I leave him now?

"Sorry I didn't tell you everything sooner."

"In your defense, you didn't keep everything from me." I yawned and checked the ancient alarm clock. "It's past midnight. I think we better get some sleep. I told Trinity to be ready by five."

"How are things going with her?"

"Surprisingly well."

He raised an eyebrow. "Really?"

"She's a beacon of information and has more secrets than all of us combined." I yawned again. "I'll have to tell you all about it later, because I desperately need to sleep." The revelations had tired me out more than sex. Although that combined with the driving probably added to my exhaustion.

"Yeah." Kenan closed the thick book and placed it on the side table. "Let's get some rest."

With his arms around me, it didn't take long to slip away from the shitty motel room and into the darkness. Too many thoughts crowded my subconscious, and I wondered if Erela would invade my dreams.

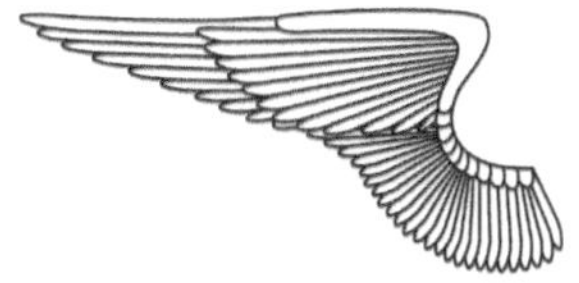

ETHEREAL INTERLUDE

The only sensation Erela the Cherubim felt was pain. The only thought able to penetrate her mind was agony.

She tried to open her eyes but even that action hurt because her endless tears had crusted them together. Her face felt coarse, as if the tears failed to replenish her skin.

Erela worried about her heart the most. Where only light and warmth filled her before, her very core had slowly transformed into a dark and barren forest. Her ribs twisted into tangled branches with spiky ends threatening to tear through her flesh.

Everything about her felt withered and old, forgotten and rotting. As if the longer she spent inside the noxious and awful room, the more her vibrant and youthful nature would be corrupted. She fretted about what she was becoming, or what would happen if the toxic environment slid below the surface.

She'd heard about the suffering of warrior angels after bloody battles with demons and humans alike. How easily their bodies changed from hardened, athletic perfection capable of withstanding all forms of attack to creatures with spindly limbs, forced to hide in the shadows of men.

How could a celestial who'd devoted her existence to protecting the innocent turn into the monster she feared? Erela might not be completely warped out of her shell yet, but she would soon become the crooked witch from fairy tales. The ones living alone, waiting until children entered her domain where she could entice them with sweets—devour their precious meat.

No, I refuse to give into hate.

Erela couldn't forget herself. She refused to become the opposite of what she'd once been. Hurting children was unfathomable. She would never allow herself to mutate into a monster.

The purest part of her goodness had been stolen in the most barbaric manner possible.

Erela felt the phantom flapping of wings at her back.

She despised the smell of brimstone lingering within the putrid walls. Hated that it was so hot her body continually dripped with sweat, but she had to push past the discomfort.

I have to go home.

The angel pried her eyes open and was glad her kind didn't have eyelashes. Her skin stung where it had come unstuck, but she blinked and the tears cleared her vision.

Red drops rained on her, dripping on her arms and legs. White feathers flew down from above. She bit down on her lip, trying to prolong what she knew had to be done as she tried to fortify herself.

Still, such precautions did nothing to stop the truth.

Erela tilted her head and sobbed.

"My poor beautiful wings."

They hung above her head from hooks and chains.

After her wings had been savagely ripped from her back, she'd passed out. The evil one must have decided to keep them there, suspended, and on display for her to see what she'd lost as soon as she awoke.

Her spine remained mercilessly numb, but she could feel the loose flaps of skin and bone whenever she moved. Even shifting an inch hurt so much her vision blurred and she collapsed again.

"Don't pass out," the childish voice said. "I need to talk to you."

She licked her lips but didn't respond, refused to give the terrible child the satisfaction. Erela was no longer pinned to the spot, but she didn't have the energy to keep her body upright, and was lying on the concrete floor with the brass cuffs and anklets providing a little wiggle room. The chains remained secured to the wall, but the length extended enough to reach the empty bucket.

Horned Lady, if you can hear me, please find me before I lose myself completely.

And she was losing herself. Her will to live slipping fast.

Yet, the Horned Lady gave her hope.

Somehow, Erela could sense her and caught glimpses of her journey. A long expanse of road, a nun as a companion, a handsome man who made her heart skip a beat.

Erela knew all these things because she saw them flash inside her mind. Could feel the demon's approach. She didn't know if the demon would arrive too late, or if she could help a celestial who'd lost her wings. But she knew the Horned Lady was honorable and determined. She wouldn't stop until she arrived at her destination.

I'm waiting for you, dear Horned Lady.

With that thought, Erela passed out and welcomed the reprieve from pain, thoughts, and reality. She also took comfort in the disgruntled huff the monstrous child made because she didn't get her way.

CHAPTER FOURTEEN

"Can you answer the door?" I called to Kenan with a mouthful of toothpaste. We were running late. *That's what happens when you spend a good chunk of the night participating in make-up sex.* And the rest getting answers to questions I wasn't sure I wanted anymore.

After hearing everything Kenan had found out about Foras and his legion, the idea of going anywhere near the demonic realm didn't have as much appeal as it used to. I'd even sent Zenda a quick text to tell her I missed her and that we were heading into the belly of the beast today. I'd almost confessed everything else, but decided those were topics better ignored or talked about in person.

The sleep I'd hoped for turned into tossing and turning and muddled messages. Blood and feathers, sorrow and agony, all of it raining down on the angel's head. Erela couldn't escape the grief, until she convinced herself she'd become a wicked monster.

Our thoughts were starting to mirror each other in the most disturbing way.

I'm waiting for you, dear Horned Lady.

I had to reach Erela because her suffering was overwhelming.

"What're you doing here?" Sister Trinity said after the rusty squeak announced Kenan had opened the door. "Where's Destiny?"

I rinsed my mouth and toothbrush.

"Good morning, Sister," Kenan said.

I left the bathroom and tucked my toothbrush into my bag. "I'm here and we're almost ready to go. Keep your habit on."

"We?" She narrowed her eyes. "He's not coming with—"

"Actually, he is." I'd surprised him with that tidbit as soon as we'd woken up because I wasn't going to leave him behind—ever. He hadn't stopped smiling since, which made him look very smug in front of the annoyed nun. "Besides, he has to come because we're taking his car."

Trinity walked away.

I liked her more than I'd expected but spending several hours away from her reminded me that no matter what, I couldn't trust her.

"She seems like great company to take on a road trip to Hell," Kenan said.

"Wait until you get to know her."

We collected our things and I followed Kenan out the door. Using his car had been his idea and I welcomed the offer because I was tired of driving. The incident with the bus had shaken me more than I wanted to admit. Besides, I didn't want to take Lady Bug into Hell.

I'd even tipped the motel clerk an extra fifty to keep her parked there for the day.

"I'll be back soon," I said, placing a hand on Lady Bug's side panel. "Behave."

"You have a strange obsession with that rust bucket," Sister Trinity said as she climbed into the backseat of Kenan's car.

"It's not obsession, it's appreciation," I said. "She does right by me and I take good care of her."

"Is that why she's all rusty?" The nun slammed the car door.

"*Rusty?* She's beautiful and it's called a patina finish, which makes her look like her namesake." No one badmouthed my car and got away with it.

"Come on, Des." Kenan sat in the driver's seat and got the engine running.

I climbed in beside him and found Kenan typing on his phone, but didn't get a chance to see who he was texting. Before I could ask, he sped out of the motel parking lot, leaving a cloud of dust in our wake.

The nun gasped and I smiled.

She had a lot to learn about Kenan's driving. He stuck to the speed limit in residential areas, but he was a fiend on highways and freeways. Yet the main reason to have him behind the wheel was so I could pay attention to our surroundings and watch out for the shed in the middle of nowhere.

I didn't remember any structures on that stretch of road. That could only mean one thing—there had to be a town nearby hidden by magic. Dark magic.

"Can you slow down?" Sister Trinity called, panicked.

"No."

I laughed. "Don't worry. He's a safe driver and he'll get us there in no time."

"In one piece?"

"Of course," I said. "Besides, we need to get there sooner than later."

"Why?" she asked.

I turned in my seat to face her. "I'm not sure if I mentioned it before, but I have a psychic connection with Erela and she won't leave me alone. She keeps sending me awful visions and won't stop popping into my dreams. She's not exactly enjoying her stay at Hotel Hell."

Trinity's eyes widened. "You forged a connection with the angel and didn't tell me?"

"To be honest, I thought Demonic Bitch might have figured it out when she trespassed into my house." I shrugged, trying to be flippant because I didn't owe her anything. "Also, I don't need to tell you everything. You're keeping plenty to yourself."

"I didn't realize such a thing was possible …"

That didn't answer if her fiendish side suspected anything, but I let it go. Blood and feathers flashed inside my mind and roused a shiver down my spine.

"Are you all right?" she asked.

"Yeah, our link is unnerving, that's all."

"Can you see what she's doing now?" Trinity asked.

I shook my head. "It doesn't work like that."

"Has this kind of thing ever happened to you before?"

"Nope. First time." *And let's hope it's also the last.*

"Being psychically linked to an angel means you're each one side of the same coin," Kenan said, keeping his eyes on the road. "It makes perfect sense, since you're both in the human realm at the moment."

"Zenda mentioned as much, but it doesn't make me feel any better."

"Then, we have to make sure we find her." He took a left turn and pointed ahead. "We're on route 666. I guess that's the highway of the beast."

"It sure is," I said. "And the shed's coming up." I turned back to the nun. "Make sure you're paying attention—all three of you."

She nodded. Her eyes flashed to white and then shifted to cream-colored, as if the three personalities were finally on the same page.

As much as Trinity got on my nerves with her pushy and lying ways, she wasn't that bad. We might have trust issues, but we were in this together.

I swiveled around and leaned against the seat. I took a deep breath of the cool air inside the vehicle. Unlike mine, Kenan's car was equipped with twenty-first century features, and while I usually didn't like the artificial nature of modern cars, I enjoyed their comfort.

Kenan sped down the road with the hot desert pressing against us. The bitumen spread far and wide as the sun slowly rose over the horizon.

A new day dawned as we headed into a situation that would probably change everything. Or we might end up spending the whole day traveling in search of a phantom town that didn't exist.

"What's that?" Sister Trinity called, bumping the back of my seat.

I opened my mouth to ask what she meant when I spotted the thick fog settling over the land on both sides of the freeway. Shadowy swirls shifted too fast to make out what was hidden inside the mist.

"Holy shit," Kennan said, ducking his head.

I looked out of the windshield and the fog engulfed us, blocking off the road. Giant wings flapped overhead, so large my heart stuttered.

"What *is* that?" I asked.

"I don't want to know," he said.

None of this happened before. I didn't remember mist or giant creatures in the sky, yet my skin itched because we were approaching the shed. I could sense its presence but couldn't see the dilapidated, half-fallen structure through the haze.

"Can you see the shed?" Kenan asked.

"I can't see anything." *But it has to be here.*

When I found Rosie, I'd dragged law enforcement with me because she was a human girl with human parents who needed proper lawful justice. Not everyone who hired us needed to find the supernatural.

"Everything feels wrong," Sister Trinity whispered but her voice carried inside the confined space.

"Even I can feel that." Kenan tightened both hands around the wheel. "My ears are buzzing."

Mine weren't, but the murmur of childish chatter and giggles echoed inside my mind, the same way it had in the motel's parking lot the night before.

"The children are too loud," the sister said.

I nodded because the noise had reached fever pitch. "I can hear them too."

"What children?" Kenan asked, giving me a quick glance.

"Too loud!" she screamed. "I wish they would stop!"

I did too.

"The shed has to be somewhere around here." I concentrated hard. My experiences on the highway from hell seemed to superimpose over each other, leading to the same spot.

"I can't see a shed," Kenan said. "Or hear any kids."

"They're too loud." The nun seemed to be struggling more than me. "It's all I can hear."

"Kenan, you have to make the turn." We had no other choice.

"Where?" he asked. "There's no road."

"Lookout!" Sister Trinity yelled from the backseat.

Kenan reacted in the nick of time when a crowd of hollow-eyed children materialized out of the fog. "Shit." He swerved and the vehicle skidded off the road. He raised his hands because he wasn't controlling the car anymore. "What the fuck is going on?"

The mist dissipated, replaced with a clear blue sky.

Kenan's car, controlled by an unseen force, bounced over the uneven terrain.

I focused on what lay ahead. From the road all we'd seen was barren land hidden by thick fog, but a town stood in the distance. A simple town consisting of a single street and several wooden structures. Every building seemed to be in a state of disrepair. I hadn't noticed this place before and wondered if it was really there. Was I pumped full of angelic fear and hallucinating? Was my mind playing tricks on me? Could Kenan and Trinity see it too?

"Do you guys see that town?" The words left my mouth before I could stop them.

"That's where we have to go," the nun said, and added, "That's where she is."

I didn't have to ask Trinity what she meant. We'd been granted access to the concealed town because Erela was waiting for me. The structures shimmered and stalled, as if the foundations were losing substance under the unnaturally bright sun.

"Kenan, go faster! We have to reach that town before it's too late," I said, trying to keep the panic from my voice.

"What town?"

"The one in front of us!" I screamed.

"There's nothing but desert," he said. "Besides, I'm not controlling the car."

"It's right *there*." I pointed out the windshield because the shine was already dimming. The chance to reach our destination was slipping away.

I didn't understand what kind of magic was at work but the town had to be hidden for a reason. Was it only visible during a certain hour of the day? Did it exist at the first touch of sunlight every morning? If we didn't hurry, the mirage might fade before we crossed the boundary.

I can feel it in my bones.

"Hurry, Kenan!"

"Des, I don't—"

Before Kenan could finish, Sister Trinity leaned over the driver's seat and gripped the steering wheel. "Hurry up," she chanted. "Hurry up!"

"Let go of the wheel, you crazy woman!"

"Don't fight her," I said.

"What?" He struggled against her, trying to push the nun off.

"Keep accelerating and let her do her thing."

I understood his confusion, but he stopped fighting against Trinity and the shed materialized in front of us.

The car slammed into the wooden slats but instead of shattering in a shower of splinters or flying into the air, we went through.

Just like the bus.

I peeked over my shoulder and found the shed still standing, intact. Had it been a ghostly formation when I'd found Rosie? It couldn't have been. I'd stepped inside with the accompanying police officers.

"She's here," Sister Trinity said, falling back into the seat. "I can feel her."

"I can feel her too." The pull in my chest unnerved me, but confirmed Erela had to be in the vicinity of that town. Her pain had projected into my dreams and the sensation of her proximity throbbed inside my core.

Trinity chanted the same thing over and over again. "She's here, she's here, she's here …"

The car slowed and stopped in front of a building that had probably operated as a store once upon a time.

"Well, that was different," Kenan said, glaring out the windshield. "Where are we?"

"You seriously couldn't see the town from the road?"

He shook his head. "There was nothing there."

My demonic influence over Kenan must not have manifested as strongly as I'd suspected, and I wasn't sure how to feel about that.

"She's here," the nun said. "I've finally found her."

"Well, it hasn't been that long." The freaky angel connection had only started a handful of days before.

She didn't reply and before I could stop her, Trinity jumped out of the car and wandered into the deserted street.

Whereas the sun had barely reached the middle of the sky on the freeway, inside the perimeter of the hidden town it hung high and bright. As if the location existed in its own plane. What kind of flying monsters were hiding in the fog? Who were those freaky kids on the road with the vacant eyes, and where had they come from? Also, why the hell had Kenan lost control of the car?

"This place feels wrong," he said, and the engine cut off. Kenan tried to restart the motor but nothing happened. "It's a veiled spot." He stared out the window. "That's why the Hellmouth is located here."

"We better catch up with Trinity before we lose her."

"Yeah, good idea." He unbuckled his seatbelt and opened the door.

"Kenan, wait a second," I said before he could get out.

"Yeah?" He turned and met my eyes.

I didn't regret bringing him along, and had to trust we would be okay. He could take care of himself and trying to protect him too fiercely had almost put an irreparable wedge between us.

"I've decided not to go anywhere," I said. "I want to stay here."

"Are you sure?"

"After considering what you found out … I don't want to risk everything I have." I took his hand and brushed my lips over his knuckles. "I'm already home. With you and Zenda, and everyone else I care about."

"And you're not going to change your mind?"

"No," I said. "It's strange that getting real answers made me realize that what I've always wanted was in front of me all along." I kissed his hand again. "I don't want to lose what I already have, especially you."

"Are you really, *totally* sure?"

"Yes," I said and released his hand. "I feel bad that you wasted your—"

"It wasn't a waste of time if it helped you make a decision." He sighed. "I just want you to be absolutely sure. Will you still feel the same way in a year? In two? Will you wonder what you've missed out on by not crossing over to at least take a peek?"

"I'm sure about this."

"I don't want to be the reason why—"

"You're not," I said. "There's a lot keeping me here. I love you and I'd be lying if I said that wasn't a big contributing factor, but when you told me about Foras and his legion … it reminded me how it felt to wake up in that alley. And what struck me the most from that memory was when Zenda found me and took me in. How she offered a confused orphan a real home and never regretted calling me her daughter. What kind of person repays such love and trust, to seek answers to questions that aren't worth asking?"

"I'll support whatever decision you make, and if you ever change your mind, I'll find another pathway. I promise." Kenan reached across the seat and brushed his lips against mine. "And Auntie would never expect to be repaid."

"I know."

Childish giggles filled the street and made my skin crawl.

"What the hell was that?"

"Those creepy kids are back," I said.

His eyes widened. "Is that what you heard before?"

"Yeah, but these kids don't sound *normal,* do they?" For starters, what would kids be doing in a town no one could see unless it wanted to be seen.

"We're in a town you won't find on any map," he said. "With a Hellmouth and an imprisoned angel. I doubt whatever we find is going to be normal by any stretch of the word."

"Let's go." I climbed out of the car and couldn't find the nun. "Where did Trinity go?"

He met me at the front of the car and surveyed the area. "I can't see her."

We stepped closer to the street and when I peered over my shoulder, the car faded from existence. Kenan followed my stare and turned as the white car vanished.

"Where did it go?"

"I don't think we should worry about that," I said. "I think we need to find the nun and the angel. Then get the fuck out of here before we disappear too."

Kenan ran a hand through his hair and nodded. "Let's find Erela."

Sometimes, the world chewed you up and spat you out. And when it did, you became damaged and wrong—evil. Sometimes, evil seeks you out. Other times, you found yourself lost inside it and wished you could get out before devastation struck.

That's exactly what stepping into this abandoned town feels like.

Every step we took into the middle of the unnatural, deserted site gave the impression of marching deeper into the belly of the beast. I felt hundreds of eyes roving over me. Hidden gazes from creatures inside the buildings and peeking around corners. Their childish giggles chased every move we made. I spotted red-glared stares from every angle, but when I turned, only the glimpse of a hand or a running shadow remained.

"This feels like a nightmare," Kenan said beside me. "Is the ground quaking under your feet? Are the buildings fading and then reappearing? I think we're stuck in the middle of the creepiest mirage ever."

"You're not wrong about the nightmare bit, but everything looks stable to me." My skin itched and when I whipped out my tail, my heart skipped a beat. *Why is my tail back?* "Can you see my tail?"

"What?" Kenan's eyes widened when he spotted the swoosh behind my rump. "Where the hell did that come from?"

I hadn't taken my medication, but that wasn't the reason why my demonic powers felt stronger than usual. Or why my tail had decided to return. A pool of rage bubbled inside the pit of my stomach like lava poised to explode and pour through my fingertips and mouth. I'd never felt my ability so close to the surface, slowly taking control.

"Are you okay?" Kenan asked, unable to hide the concern.

"Why?"

"Your eyes are glowing red."

"They are?" My sight wasn't blurred by a red haze, and hadn't thinned out to horizontal view like it used to do when my fury reached its peak. Yet something had definitely changed.

"I've never seen you with red eyes." He seemed intrigued, rather than repulsed.

"Don't get too close because I don't understand what's going on."

Kenan took a step closer.

Heat rushed over my skin and started to melt my clothes.

"What the hell's happening?" I backed away from Kenan as my jeans melted to reveal my hairy legs and cloven hooves. The entire length shifted into the bent goat legs I'd lost years ago. My top spun away like glitter, dissolved to reveal a thick layer of scarlet skin. "What's happening to me?"

"Your true self must be taking over." Kenan couldn't stop staring, seemed fascinated by the transformation. "The proximity of the Hellmouth and the infernal influence of this town must be affecting you."

"What does that mean?" I spread my arms and noticed thick ruby skin covering my chest, stomach, and hands. Long black nails tipped my fingers.

"It means that the longer you spend in our world, the more your demonic attributes have disappeared."

"Because of the glamour?"

"Yes, no, sort of." He shook his head. "Maybe it's a combination of the glamour's potency, but I think it's more to do with the actual amount of time you spend in the human world."

"Do you think there's a chance that I might eventually become completely human?"

"I'm not sure." A smile spread over his lips. "But I'd be happy to accept your query as my next research challenge. I would love to find out what effects hanging around humans has on my girlfriend."

"Your girlfriend?" Considering these awful changes, it seemed silly to be caught off guard by such a simple word.

"What would you prefer that I call you? Lover? Companion?"

"Girlfriend sounds fine for now." I wanted to be happy about this new development, but my body distracted me. Everything—inside and out—felt alien and familiar. "Has my face changed?"

"No. Only your eyes and your shiny reddish skin have." He circled around me and whistled. "You're beautiful. Stunning."

I'd never thought about it before, but I wondered if Kenan was right about my diminishing demonic attributes being influenced by the humans around me. It made sense. If they were affected by me, I had to be affected by *them*. If I lost my hooves and horns completely, would Kenan still find me attractive? I could see the lust burning in his gaze. Shifting into a hideous version of myself appealed to him. Like Zenda, he'd never been disgusted by my features.

The giggling intensified.

We were surrounded by children and dolls. Every single one— whether flesh or plastic—had vacant white sockets and a ring of black around their eyes. I tasted the brimstone emanating off their small shells and the demonic influence chased over my skin like poison I wanted to inject directly into my bloodstream.

All of the little monsters were possessed by a formidable entity. I could sense the oily influence in their small bodies like parasites controlling puppets.

I tried to zero in further, much like I used to do with people's souls, past the murky exteriors and the deep influence. Attempting to extricate their essence. I found nothing. These children had become husks, and had reanimated dolls by tapping into the demon's influence.

"What the hell do they want?" Kenan asked. "They remind me of Mylings."

"Of what?"

"The ghosts of unbaptized children who jump weary travelers and demand to be buried properly," he said with a shrug. As if this should be common knowledge. "Or black-eyed kids."

"No way to check the unbaptized bit, but these kids don't want to be buried," I said. "I'm pretty sure they're more interested in burying us."

The ones near the front hissed like rabid animals and I spotted rows of tiny sharp teeth and wretched skin. The fine cracks spread over their features.

"Stay close to me." I took Kenan's hand, pushed him behind me, and wrapped my tail around his midsection. He didn't resist my newfound strength.

The swarm of kids and dolls shambled closer. Short legs pounded against the hard dirt and small feet rushed forward.

"What do we do?"

"Stay close," I said.

"What're you planning?"

"I have to get rid of these pests."

"Oh, shit." He nestled against my spine and tightened his grip on my hand.

I squeezed my tail around his waist and he grunted.

Caught in the momentum and frenzy, the children ran for us and their dolls lurched like rickety robots. Every single creepy monster seemed intent on closing the distance and their cracked limbs advanced fast.

It took every shred of willpower I possessed to concentrate on what I had to do while protecting Kenan.

I slowed my breathing and the fire beneath my skin turned my blood to lava, swishing inside to form a raging volcano. I considered our surroundings. I fixed all my concentration on the pool of fury stirring within. I'd never attempted to open more than one pentagram void. But in my current state, on a forgotten street, I believed myself to be strong enough to do just that.

"Come on, you little freaks. Come closer."

The kids and dolls ate the distance, and when the ground opened up in a line of interlocked blazing pentagrams that formed a pitch-black circle between us and them, the small runts tumbled into the darkness beneath with their animated dolls on their heels.

Kenan pressed his body against mine.

I widened the ring.

The kids dropped like dominoes, but didn't stop advancing. Instead, toppled into the void, lemmings who couldn't control their movements because they worked in tandem.

I couldn't help but smile as their numbers diminished quickly. I felt a satisfaction I hadn't experienced before during a pentagram opening. I wanted the possessed kids to fall to their deaths. In some fucked up way, my cruelty would be a mercy to these husks.

"Holy shit!" Kenan yelled near my ear. "I think you got all of them!"

I lowered the level of energy exuding from within and shrank the circle. The abyss shriveled as the gritty ground knitted itself back together near my hooves.

"Almost done," I whispered.

"Des!"

Mischievous sniggering drowned out Kenan's voice and I spun around.

"They got me!" Kenan kicked their small hands but too many shiny eyes glowed inside the chasm and sharp-nailed fingers held on. Tiny digits tore through his jeans and drew blood. The harder he fought, the more he slipped.

"No!" I yanked, tried to drag Kenan from their grasp with my tail but it unwound from around his waist. I snatched both of his hands and pulled until my shoulders ached.

His eyes filled with fear, but also resignation. "Let go, Des."

I shook my head while trying to reopen the pentagram void, but I couldn't. The hole got smaller by the second and if I didn't let him go, Kenan would be cut in half.

"You have no choice," he whispered.

Our hands were damp with sweat.

The flames below rose too high.

"Des, it's okay."

"It's not!" Nothing would ever be okay if I lost Kenan. I tightened my grip but the creepy fucks weighed him down.

"I love you," he whispered.

"I love you too," I said. "I'm not going to let you …"

My fingers slid from his and Kenan fell.

The possessed children held onto him. They'd taken Kenan with them into the pit.

All I could do was watch the expression of resignation on Kenan's face a second before the abyss sealed, and entombed him forever.

I collapsed to my knees and punched both fists against the packed dirt in a desperate attempt to reopen the void.

"No!" The heat and the spark burning inside me had diminished. "Come back!"

What am I going to do?

Our story couldn't end with tragedy. Not after the turmoil of the last few days. Not after finally confessing our true feelings. And definitely not after I'd decided to stay with him.

We were meant to be together.

"I'll find you!" I yelled and my voice echoed down the godforsaken street. Even if it was the last thing I ever did, I'd find Kenan and bring him back.

"He's gone," a familiar voice said behind me. "I'm sorry."

Sister Trinity put a hand on my shoulder and in spite of myself, I placed mine over hers and wept until I felt hollow.

CHAPTER FIFTEEN

"Destiny, I can see that you're grieving, but we have to finish what we started." Sister Trinity broke the uncanny stillness. "We have to keep going."

Sulfur hung thick in the air.

The energy I'd exuded to send those little runts to wherever the hell the void ended hadn't taken as much energy as losing Kenan. The thought of him winding up in the same place as those freaks terrified me. What would happen to him? Who would find him? And most importantly, how could I get him back?

I'll do whatever it takes.

I sniffed, but didn't have to wipe the tears because my heated skin dried them as they fell. With the nun's help, I stood and turned to face her.

"Where did you go?" I couldn't hide my anger. She hadn't been there when the kids appeared. Trinity's lies were starting to take a toll. That she'd helped the lost souls on the freeway didn't excuse her from everything.

"What happened?" Sister Trinity looked me in the eye. "All I saw was Kenan …"

I winced at the reminder, could still see his face as he surrendered to the inevitable.

"Trinity, where were you?"

"Looking for her."

That she chose not to answer my question bugged me, but I didn't push. Too many conflicting emotions stirred inside me and the main one was finishing the job.

Then I could find the Hellmouth and get to the other side.

I wasn't leaving without Kenan. And now that I knew the name of my legion's leader, I had no doubt his domain was where all the unfortunate spirits I sent on their way probably ended up. What would Foras do with them? Probably the usual demonic thing—use their essence for fuel and snacks.

Some demonic tropes didn't hold up, but others were factual.

I sighed. "Did you find Erela?"

"This way." Sister Trinity took a few steps and stopped. She glared at the building in front of us—a wooden structure much like the others. Except an odd pulse emanated from inside.

A source of energy that made my hair stand on end.

"Hey, what's going on?" I sidled up beside the nun and spotted an ashy blonde girl peeking around the side of the building. Like the other kids, her white eyes were rimmed in black, but this kid wore an unnerving and mischievous smirk on her pale face. As if she was hiding something. "Who the hell is that?"

Why does she look familiar?

Sister Trinity raised her left hand as she advanced, as if trying to contain a wild animal. The recognition concerned me, and when her eyes switched from brown to white and cream-colored as easily as switching channels, a sense of doom spread over me.

Her shoulders shook and her head tilted sideways in an unnatural way. She wrapped her right hand around the rosary. Her skin sizzled at the contact but she didn't react. The farther she got from me, the less Trinity resembled the nun I'd become familiar with.

"It's okay, Eden," she whispered.

"Eden? You recognize this girl?"

"Of course, I do." She turned to flash me a wicked smile. The kind I hadn't seen on her face since the day we'd met. "A mother always recognizes her child."

"What did you say?" I couldn't believe my ears. Surely, I'd misheard her. In what way could this girl be Sister Trinity's child? Did she mean it in the sense of all children being a part of God and therefore hers? There was no other way to interpret such a claim. Nuns didn't have children.

"Eden is my daughter."

"But how?"

"That doesn't matter." She took another step. "You already know it's true. You've seen Eden before."

The nun and the young girl holding hands. Trinity tried to exorcise the demon, only to have the child infect her instead. She wasn't properly trained or equipped to deal with a demonic possession.

It suddenly made sense. Sister Trinity had a personal stake in the girl and that was why she'd risked her own life.

"This is the kid who infected you."

"She is."

"That's why you were invested in helping her." My head spun as the pieces fell into place. "She's your daughter and the Church wouldn't help … then you took it upon yourself. And instead, made everything worse."

"It wasn't her fault." Trinity stood too close to Eden.

"Don't get any closer to her." I didn't like the malevolent tremors gushing from the kid. Unlike the other freaks I'd sent sailing into oblivion, this one seemed to be made of malice and smoke. She had to be patient zero, the one who brought hell into the town and wiped it off the literal map.

"She means me no harm."

Trinity's admission made me realize the truth.

"You never cared about Erela, did you? The angel served as a convenient excuse to find Eden. A way to seek us out without having to provide the real reason because you wanted to keep your daughter a secret. You've lied from the beginning and haven't stopped." I felt like such a fool. I'd started liking her during our long drive to the motel, especially after she released the trapped spirits inside the bus. "I don't get it. You could've told us the truth and we still would've tried to find her."

"You never would've found Eden directly." The nun's shoulders trembled and her voice developed a disturbing echo. "She's too far gone. She's barely a child anymore, there's nothing left. Phenex took everything."

Phenex. Why did that name ring a bell?

"Trinity, you still could've told us about the demon, I—"

"You're capable of finding a great many things." She turned her head until her neck bent in an unnatural angle. The disturbing white eyes drilled right through me. "But you can't find a demon who's in hiding. One who can infect a single child. Multiply her into a hundred and then conceal himself."

"You don't know what I'm capable of." Although Trinity might be right. During my vision, I'd gotten the location but hadn't seen any trace of a town. Only the road and the shed—no buildings or a hidden demon, not even a bunch of dead kids.

"Destiny, you've been here before. Yet, you didn't notice the demon's influence."

I swallowed the lump in my throat because I understood what she meant. Phenex had embedded himself into the very soil to conceal their existence, and that included cloaking the girl.

The angel had provided an anchor.

Sister Trinity wanted to find Erela because the celestial would lead her to Eden.

"You used me," I said. "You fucking used me!" The theatrics, secrets and lies … every morsel was a way to control my motivations.

The nun had almost reached her daughter but her head twisted all the way around, watching me. Eden raised a small hand and their fingers inched closer.

I knew they would connect in seconds and had no idea what would happen. Yet I didn't move. I observed the interaction, fascinated by the bizarre scene unfolding in front of me.

"Yes, I used you," Sister Trinity said. "I knew that a guardian angel falling from grace would provide a reason to hire you, and make a worthwhile offering for Phenex. I figured out you could get me inside the town back when I planted Rosie years ago. But you had to bring the humans in, didn't you?" She spat on the ground. "The presence of police officers ensured Hell wouldn't reveal itself, but I was patient."

"Wait a minute," I snapped. "You killed an innocent kid to bring me here?"

"I didn't have to kill her," she said with a shake of her head. "The Great Marquis Phenex took care of that. I just found her while trying to reach Eden."

"I can't believe what I'm hearing."

"Mothers do whatever it takes to keep their children safe." Trinity sighed and she sounded sad but not remorseful. "I wanted to find Eden to get her out of here, but Phenex has embedded himself into both of us."

"You used an angel as a tool. And used me as a weapon for your own quest." She'd taken advantage of my demonic nature to get her to the only damned destination that mattered to her, so I could find her lost daughter.

"I did what I had to do." Trinity's fingers joined with her daughter's and a blast of noxious smoke spread behind them.

A sweet melody started, a lullaby eager to burn itself into my brain.

I scanned the deserted street and didn't find any other cretins around. Where was the music coming from?

The nun and the girl held hands as Trinity's head righted itself and she swiveled around. Mother and daughter glared at me like a pair of ivory-eyed creatures hell-bent on destroying everything in their path.

"I can finally ascend to take my place on the Seventh Throne." Their mouths enunciated the words together but their voices morphed into the one I'd heard in Erela's nightmares.

They're conduits.

"Phenex, is that you?" I dared to ask.

"It is." A fiery silhouette rose above the possessed mother and daughter. Barely there, but substantial enough to recognize the phoenix. Matching crimson orbs rose into the sky.

I couldn't help but think of Zenda's shadow bird. The presence of this demon had a similar—yet more subdued—influence than Spark. I understood what that meant, but chose not to dwell on it.

"What do you really want with me?" Trinity's distorted reasons didn't provide the whole story, demons always had ulterior motives. If Phenex targeted a nun to discover her deepest secret, steal it and then use the child as bait, there had to be a much bigger picture.

The woman and girl grinned as smoke surrounded their bodies. "You're the daughter of President Foras. You're a very valuable pawn in my endless quest."

"I'm no daughter, just part of his legion."

The smoky phoenix wavered as it swelled, but the conduits' eyes narrowed and a horrid cackle filled the air.

"You might be a demon, but you're as dumb as any human. You're his daughter. A member of the Hellish court, the one who will ascend his throne. How could you not know? Did you honestly think a common minion possessed your abilities? No, only an offspring could do everything you've proven you can achieve." Their eyes narrowed and scrutinized me. The way mother and child mirrored each other disturbed me but made sense because the pair were being controlled by a demonic puppet master. "You were a threat to him, so he got rid of you."

Listening to the demon talk about my former life, as if he had a right to, made my skin crawl, but I kept my feelings at bay. "I appreciate the history lesson, but can you tell me where the angel is? I need to rescue her and I'll be on my way."

I was done playing games.

First, I'd found out I happened to be a minion inside a dingy motel room. Now, according to a demonic in hiding, I was supposedly a president's daughter. I had no interest in finding out where I fit into the hierarchy of Hell, and especially didn't care about the desires of the demon before me.

His cackle roused a shiver down my spine.

"The angel is almost expired, and is my offering along with all the others. And you."

"You kept their essence." It wasn't a question, yet another realization. "How could you do such a thing?" That explained the hollowed-husk kids. I'd sent dead flesh into the void. On one hand, I felt relieved. But it also meant Kenan was the only soul who'd tumbled into my abyss of darkness.

I really need to get him out of there.

"Sometimes, we do the strangest things to get back home, don't we?" Trinity and Eden's heads tilted closer, almost touching. "You of all people should understand."

My fury returned and stirred in the pit of my stomach. The lava I'd thought was spent bubbled inside, rose up my esophagus and tickled the back of my throat. Threatened to spill from my mouth at any moment.

I took a shallow breath and exhaled a ring of smoke. If I wasn't careful, I'd ruin my surprise. I had one chance, because the demon wasn't going to let me save Erela and walk away. I might not defeat the Great Marquis but I had to get the other two freaks out of the way. And since Trinity and Eden were linked to Phenex, maybe …

Hopefully, being locked up and hidden inside a forgotten town had weakened the marquis. The fact Phenex spoke about souls as if spirits functioned separately, made me think they might be stored somewhere else.

Phenex had split himself into too many pieces, I doubted the demon possessed the strength to realistically threaten me.

"I apologize for what I must do," they said together, and I could've sworn the nun's voice spoke beneath the demon's. "But adding your essence to the potent mix I've collected will secure everything I've fought to regain."

"It's not going to be that easy."

"We'll see."

The nun and her daughter rushed me.

Holding hands, their dead eyes glared into mine as the two advanced like soldiers into battle. The same way the swarm had done before I'd obliterated every single runt. But these two were accompanied by an awful lullaby scraping at my brain—and the growing shadow of the demon who'd possessed them.

I held my breath to keep the power stifled until they got closer, and exhaled when I opened the pentagram void.

The two approached too fast, and neither had the opportunity to stop their determined march.

Trinity and Eden plunged into the darkness, and took the stupid jingle with them.

"Have fun meeting Foras!"

I breathed in the waft of steam from below, while slowly releasing my grip on the opening.

A pale hand reached out of the chasm and wrapped around my leg, dragging me down to the ground. I landed on something hard and pushed it away, only to recognize the sulfuric stone.

Vibrating.

It must have fallen out of my pocket when the jeans burned off my body. I had to get rid of it.

"Shit." I kicked the hand away with my other hoof until the nun fell into the pit. The last thing I heard from within the darkness was the dual scream from the nun and her child as they fell to oblivion.

The shadow of the phoenix flew out of the opening like a puff of smoke with matching crimson orbs. But was inhaled into the crevice when I tossed the yellow rock into the pit.

I held my breath until the crater sealed completely.

When the ground leveled out, my thoughts twisted into a warped and confused mess.

Sending Sister Trinity into the abyss was the last thing I'd expected to do, and actually shed a few tears. In spite of her deception, it wasn't the nun's fault that she'd become a demented entity.

The Church let her down with its rigid rules and the demon had broken her into tiny pieces. She'd never had a chance.

At least she might finally find peace with her daughter.

"You're right, she finally found what she was looking for," someone said.

I kicked at the dirt and got up so quickly my head spun. "What the hell?" Just when I thought this nightmare might be over, another decided to crash the party. "I thought ..."

"Don't worry," Sister Trinity said with a serene smile that clashed with the crisscrossed scars on her face. "She's really gone."

"Then what are *you* doing here?" She wasn't quite sentient because I could see through her, but I recognized her cream-colored eyes and calming nature. The part of Sister Trinity who'd saved the bus full of spirits lingered behind.

"I'm not like the other two." She focused on the ground between us. "I was Trinity's guardian angel and forced myself inside her when she was possessed. I couldn't let her battle the demon alone."

"She was carrying a demon *and* an angel?"

She nodded.

"No wonder she was unstable."

"Yes, but my journey is almost over." The best part of Sister Trinity floated across the street and stopped at the door of the quivering building. "You have to open the door and let them out."

"What are they?" Were the pulsations voices calling out to anyone who could hear them?

"You've already worked that out."

I nodded, because somehow, I had. "And you'll release their spirits like you did before, on the freeway?"

"No." She pressed her hands together in prayer. "She's waiting. I'll lead them to her."

My heart didn't slow as I limped across the dirt towards her. She had to be talking about Erela. The closer I got, the more the building glowed and called to me in a visceral way that caused the sensations of loss and need to race over my skin. My ears filled with frenetic energy. Could the spirits detect my approach, or did the nun's guardian affect them?

"Go ahead," she whispered.

A sense of peace washed over me, soothing the nerves I'd accumulated since the ordeal began. I wasn't sure what to expect on the other side of the wooden door and when I pushed it open, the shimmering baubles made my eyes water.

I shielded my face with a hand.

The spirits of all the children Phenex had stolen via a possessed girl were stored inside. Luminescent baubles flew outside and followed the nun. Their radiance lit up the abandoned town with a sparkle of color shinier than the sun.

A beautiful rainbow of imprisoned souls in search of freedom.

"Holy shit." I couldn't believe my eyes, but clomped down the uneven stairs after them, and didn't stop until the cavalcade reached a barn off the main path.

When I stepped closer, I spotted the faint outlines of small faces inside each bauble.

"It's almost time," Sister Trinity's angelic spirit said.

I'm waiting for you, dear Horned Lady.

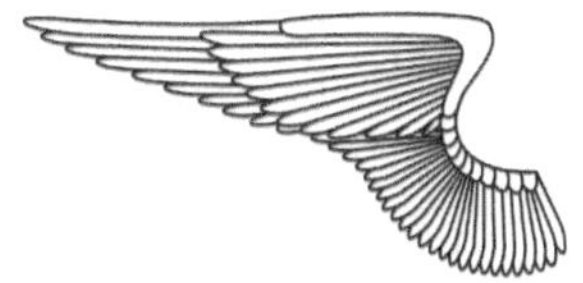

ETHEREAL INTERLUDE

Erela woke with a start and tore the crusty sand from her eyes when they snapped open. She'd expected to find the horrid girl watching and waiting in the shadows of the filthy room. Instead, she was alone but restrained by the chains and brass rings around her wrists and ankles. The metal had rubbed away her skin and she could see white bone peeking through.

The lethargy spread like a virus.

Still, she persisted and managed to sit up. Aside from the filth and brimstone, nothing had changed. The empty bucket was tipped on its side. Blood and feathers continued to rain down. Everything hurt.

A sudden, collective holler of spirits crammed her mind with sorrow.

Erela collapsed onto the concrete as the shrieks tore through her weak body. Children. All of them affected in some terrible way. And she couldn't help, could barely even move.

At least the intrusion confirmed she hadn't completely lost herself.

If Erela heard and felt children nearby, then she hadn't become the gnarled and cruel woman from the woods. She remained a Cherub who helped keep children safe and was a part of them as much as they were a part of her.

Yet a dark disturbance hung in the air.

A new presence had arrived.

Erela recognized the Horned Lady, sensed her nearby. She was the one causing the vibration of havoc. The reason why the earth quaked beneath her. Did that mean she'd defeated the monster who'd been keeping Erela captive? Would the demon help Erela break free of her captivity? But even if she got away, how would she survive without wings?

Erela tilted her head and watched blood and feathers rain from above. Her detached wings would never stop bleeding and couldn't be reattached, but she craved their cocoon of safety.

The stumps on the backs of her shoulders stung and spasmed in response to the missing limbs.

Shattering metal made her jump.

Familiar spirits made her skin itch.

A sudden breeze swept around her body, filling Erela's heart with joy when she recognized the wave of color tearing into the room. Her eyes were dazzled by the rainbow tornado.

She hovered over the concrete and relished the mad rush.

"Come to me, my children," she whispered and spread her arms.

The wave of souls smacked into Erela's chest and one by one, each lost spirit imprisoned in the horrible town engulfed her frame.

The brass restraints melted and the chains clinked to the ground.

Erela understood the fear and torment, witnessed when every single spirit was stolen from suburbs and towns by the possessed Pied Piper who befriended them. A horrid girl who infected the other children with her writhing darkness and brought them to this hellish place.

Forever lost, their essences were split from their flesh. Separated from their shells for too long, the spirits had finally found their way to the safety and warmth of the celestial who could protect them.

When Erela's feet touched the ground, all her ailments faded and she felt strong and radiant.

The radiance engulfed her completely and she whispered, "It's time to go home."

"I won't be able to get you and your entourage home, but I can get you out of this dump."

Erela turned her attention to the demon from her thoughts.

The Horned Lady stood across the room and she was beautiful. Long dark wavy hair caught in her majestic horns, and a sleek tail whipped out behind her. Even her hardened crimson arms, upper body, and hairy animalistic legs added to the stunning picture.

Everything about the demon radiated brighter than anything she'd encountered above.

The demon had released the children and allowed them to find their way to salvation.

Erela blinked to ensure she wasn't suffering another delusion, but the demon didn't disappear. And a nun's spirit shadowed her. What was left of the damaged human nun was driven by a fragmented guardian angel.

She dipped her chin at the fellow wisp of an angel, who returned the acknowledgment.

"You came," she whispered to the demon. "It's nice to finally meet you, Horned Lady."

"I would call you Winged One, but"—she motioned at the ceiling—"that would be cruel. I'll just stick to Erela, and you can call me Destiny."

"Destiny?"

"Yeah."

"It seems fitting, since you've proven to be *my* destiny." As soon as the words tumbled out of her mouth, Erela doubled over.

Although the pain rippled down her spine, she smiled.

CHAPTER SIXTEEN

Strange how I seemed to fit the destiny role for a lot of people, yet usually felt like an inadequate failure. I'd failed the one person I loved the most. Losing Kenan left a hole in my heart that I hoped to refill when I got him back. Because I was going to get him back, even if I had to go to Hell to do it.

I packed the thought away for later while I struggled to accept what was going on inside the dingy room I'd seen in my dreams.

The luminosity seared into my corneas. The spirits had somehow entered the guardian, and she'd grown a new pair of wings. The new limbs stretched out behind her rail-thin body. The shimmer of white feathers seemed out of place inside a filthy prison. The tips hit the walls on either side, but she didn't seem to care.

Erela's smile widened. She was tall and I had to crane my neck to admire her ethereal face. Her shaggy silver hair was made of small feathers and her cream-colored eyes reminded me of Sister Trinity. Where had the ghost gone? Erela wasn't wearing any clothes because her whole body was covered in soft ivory feathers that stopped under her chin and jaw. Her spindly legs ended in clawed feet.

She resembled a bird more than anything I'd ever seen in the scriptural depictions of angels, which made sense. A demon like me was caprine and an angel like her was avian.

"Thank you," she sang, and her sweet voice sounded more like a melody. She looked nothing like the ruined shell I'd found on the floor after snapping the brass padlock on the iron door. Erela had sat, a pale and bloody shriveled insect without wings. Now she was majestic and glowing from the inside out—illuminated by all the spirits she'd consumed.

I couldn't help but stare at the wings secured by chains above our heads. "I'm sorry about those."

"It's not your fault," she said. "Besides, I've got new ones."

"Did you suspect that would happen?"

Erela shrugged. "No, and if it hadn't been for you releasing all of these innocent souls, I probably wouldn't have regrown new wings."

"You're welcome." I stood across from the statuesque angel in awe of her majestic presence. "Can you find your way home?"

She nodded and even that motion reminded me of a bird. "I can."

"Good." I sighed. "What will happen to them?" It seemed a shame to leave her wings hanging there.

"As soon as I leave this room, they'll wither away."

I accepted her answer with a nod. Sister Trinity's angelic ghost appeared underneath the bleeding wings. "And what about her?"

"She'll join us." Erela tilted her head as if trying to read my mind. "The good parts of Trinity survived because of her guardian and you."

I couldn't interpret any of the miraculous bullshit, but her words made me feel safe and cozy.

"I appreciate what you've done to revitalize and bring me back from the brink of oblivion." Erela plucked a shiny ivory feather from her left wing. "And for that, I want you to have this."

I took the silky offering and my fingers buzzed because the feather hummed like a living thing. "Thanks."

"I'm a guardian and a protector," Erela chanted. "My specialty might be children, but you, my Destiny, have definitely earned my protection." She lowered her head. "I owe you a great debt."

"No, it's fine, really—"

Her eyes widened. "Where you're going, you'll need all the protection you can get. As long as you keep this part of me with you at all times, you'll remain invisible in Hell."

"Really?"

"Yes." Erela brushed her cool fingers against my temples and closed her eyes. "Keep the feather close and no one will sense your presence. Go to the summoning chamber, find your lost love and help will be waiting for you."

"Okay." What wondrous instructions were these? I had no idea what a summoning chamber was, how I would find Kenan or who could possibly be there to pull me out. But I trusted this angel.

Erela dropped her hand. "But you must remember this one very important instruction."

"What's that?"

"You have only one quest to fulfil by entering the Hellmouth. Go to the summoning chamber, rescue what's yours and don't try to find out anything else. Don't wonder about your origins or get anyone's attention. And don't look back when you leave."

Her enigmatic directions echoed in my ears and seemed to settle inside my mind.

"The answers you seek have already found you and very soon, you'll remember exactly how you came to be in this world." Erela smiled.

Hissing distracted me and hummed over my body. Although her mouth was still moving, I couldn't hear a thing Erela was saying.

I stepped back while trying to figure out where the noise and sensation was coming from, wondered why it affected me when no one else seemed to hear it. I inhaled sulfur tinged with a cloying sweetness that pushed deep into my brain. Neurons ignited and the undeniable sensation of heat bubbled beneath the surface.

"You've found it?" the angel asked from somewhere.

I didn't answer—*couldn't.*

The only thing that mattered was getting closer to the hidden corner in the room, where a smoky doorway had appeared. Flames flickered within and I knew it wasn't a furnace or a fireplace. With Erela's guidance, I'd located the Hellmouth Kenan had told me about.

My point of entry, where I could return to the realm of the demonic to find the man I loved and bring him back home.

I have no idea how I can do this, or if it's even possible, but this will get me there.

A cool hand on my shoulder startled me and the bubble of concentration broke. I spun around to face the feathered angel.

I licked my lips. "I found a Hellmouth."

"Yes, you did. I can't see it, but feel it through you."

I nodded because I was all out of snark and kept repeating her instructions inside my mind over and over again. I didn't want to forget a single one.

"You have only one quest to fulfil by entering the Hellmouth. Go to the summoning chamber, rescue what's yours and don't try to find out anything else. Don't wonder about your origins or get anyone's attention. And don't look back when you leave."

"Go and find your handsome man." Erela's voice soothed me and a cocoon of safety enveloped my body. Her advice and the feather were going to help me find Kenan, because she was right about that too.

I'd already decided I wasn't interested in going anywhere, but without Kenan … no place would ever feel like home.

I'm coming for you.

"Erela, I'm really glad I found you." Ending up in a forsaken town turned out to be a nightmare I couldn't wait to escape, but I'd never forget the experience. "How will you get back to uh, Heaven? And what will happen to this town?"

I clutched the feather.

"Don't worry about me, I'll be fine. As for this wretched town, it will fade from existence. You need to go and find your place in the world." The flames from the pathway reflected in her eyes. "And if you ever need me, use the feather to call me. I'll listen out and will watch over you. Our connection will never be severed. We're friends for all eternity."

Before I had a chance to say anything else, Erela the Cherubim pushed me into Hell.

Chapter Seventeen

Sinking into a fiery well wasn't painful or scary, though I lost all sense of direction because I kept spinning. The thick smoke smudged my vision and I could feel countless hands reaching out from within the flames, and heard the endless moans.

The way to Hell is paved with souls.

Inside the darkness, I was Alice falling into my own version of Wonderland. The idea excited and terrified me.

After spending most of my life carrying abandonment issues because I was summoned and left to die, the need to find out where I came from had lost its luster. I was nervous and worried about whether I would make it, or worse—get trapped. What if I didn't find Kenan? What if I couldn't find my way home to Zenda?

The angel's faith in me provided solace but not confidence.

At least Erela had regained the majestic qualities that made her a creature of light. A multitude of innocent souls were no longer trapped inside a dingy building in a horrible town. And the best piece of Sister Trinity was saved.

My adventure, since the ridiculous request to find an angel had first swamped my life a handful of days ago, had led to the place I'd been hoping Kenan would help me find. And when he had, I'd denounced the need to return. Yet I was heading there to get *him* out.

I fell backwards, down the strange tunnel to a destination I didn't remember. I wasn't angry with Erela for pushing me through because in a sense, it confirmed I'd been on the right track all along.

The feather tucked in my hair provided a sense of safety.

Hope she's right about making me invisible.

No matter what I found in Foras's territory, I had to keep a low profile. Kenan claimed I was part of a legion and that made me a random minion. But the demon who'd possessed Trinity and Eden, the Great Marquis Phenex, referred to me as an heir. If that was true, how would the president react to my unexpected return? Would he detect my return?

The answer wasn't as important as finding Kenan and going home. Getting there was one thing, but getting out was another. Still, I had to trust Erela knew what she was talking about when she made this quest appear simple.

My spine struck a rocky surface and caught me off guard. But my tough exterior lessened the brunt of the impact.

It took me a few seconds to get my breath back and clear the blotches in my vision that simultaneously hitting spine and skull had produced. I studied the high ceiling above me, and whatever tunnel I'd fallen through had disappeared. I'd landed inside a cave or some sort of chamber.

I sat up and groaned. The impact vibrated through every muscle. I rubbed the back of my skull and sighed. At least the smell of brimstone and sulfur perked me up.

Muttering voices came out of nowhere and I stood.

I didn't see anyone but the murmurs seemed to be coming from everywhere.

On closer inspection, the floor might have been made of sharp rock but the walls were shiny obsidian. The sigil Kenan pointed out in the old book had been etched all over the place in different sizes. I recognized part of the pattern from one of the charms I'd carried with me when I was summoned to the human realm.

I ran my fingertips over the lines and curves. Tracing the sigils drew energy from the wall and it stirred deep inside my belly. I pulled my hand back when the sigils lit up with an orange glow that brought the room to life. Was this some kind of temple or throne room?

The sharp intake of breath made me realize I wasn't alone.

A stone altar positioned in the middle of the vast area, with dark stains dripping down the grooves on all four sides, had a prone figure stretched over it. Someone I recognized instantly.

"Kenan!" I rushed to his side and ran my fingertips over his face in an attempt to wake him. "Kenan."

His heart was still beating and his breath was steady. He wasn't restrained. But how had he ended up inside the chamber? Did my pentagram void dump everyone in the same place? And why was he laid out?

The chatter continued around me, humming inside my skull and getting louder and stronger. Bouncing off the walls and into my ears. No matter how hard I tried to focus, I couldn't catch a single word and was convinced most weren't even in English.

"You have only one quest to fulfil by entering the Hellmouth. Go to the summoning chamber, rescue what's yours and don't try to find out anything else. Don't wonder about your origins or get anyone's attention. And don't look back when you leave."

Erela's words brought me back to myself. I didn't have the time to worry about who was talking and why. Or what purpose such a strange chamber served, and whether it had anything to do with me. I'd come here to find Kenan.

"Kenan," I whispered near his lips. "Please, wake up." I dropped my head on his chest and listened to the steady thump-thump.

I might have the angel's feather tucked away and found the man I loved, but none of that mattered if he wasn't conscious and we couldn't escape.

"Wake up." I brushed my lips against his for the softest touch, hoping for a fairy tale miracle.

His eyes fluttered.

"Kenan?"

The wall across from where I stood parted and a huge horned demon with hard magenta skin and goat legs entered the chamber. His massive body reminded me of a beefy bodybuilder. The bulging muscles on his thighs spasmed with every step. His bald head nearly hit the tall ceiling, and every heavy stomp made the ground rumble beneath me.

"Is the offering ready?" he asked, stepping inside with a much smaller demon trailing him.

"He is." The second horned demon walked past the giant and he paled in comparison.

"Did you get rid of those disgusting husks?"

"Yes, sir. I fed their rotting shells to the minions." The smaller one motioned at Kenan. "This was the only one worth keeping."

At least he'd confirmed the handful of *people* who'd fallen through my pentagram void ended up inside this chamber. I couldn't help but wonder if Oki's husband had also found himself lying on the sacrificial altar.

The walls sealed behind the demons and the sigils blazed.

"What is that smell?" The massive demon frowned, sniffing the air with huge nostrils. "Why are the sigils lit already?"

"I'm not sure, President." The smaller demon considered Kenan's prone body. "It's probably the human. You know how bad they smell."

"It's not him." The giant made his way farther into the chamber and studied the stone altar Kenan was lying on. "I can feel another presence."

"I don't feel anything."

"Of course you don't," he barked. "That's why I'm the master and you're the sacrificial minion."

My pulse drummed inside my temples and I sent a silent prayer to the feather. *Please, please conceal us from this monster.* The smaller guy referred to him as President. Was he Foras? He definitely exuded the pompous air of grandeur expected from an infernal ruler, but I couldn't remember him.

I had no way of confirming if I was related to either demon.

Having the president close was playing havoc with my mind and spirit. I tried to ignore the sensation, but his presence suffocated me, and I didn't understand why.

I wanted to reveal myself, challenge him to see if he recognized me. Needed to understand why I felt drawn to him. Could Phenex have been right? Was President Foras my father? He had two sets of large goat horns on the sides of his head and several smaller ones running in vertical rows over his bald scalp. The face might have been somewhat humanoid and he even had a goatee, but the brute was made entirely of crocodile hide and carried a lot of strength. Not to mention he was more Titan than demon.

"I feel an air of familiarity ..." His voice trailed off as he rubbed his goatee.

"The room is ready for you," the minion said. "That's probably what you feel. The summoners are all speaking at once, but soon the loudest and most needy will reveal themselves and you can claim their soul."

"Yes, yes." The giant seemed distracted as he strolled around Kenan's sprawled body. True to her word, the feather in my hair kept me from his line of sight. He stopped in front of me, but he couldn't see me.

The opposite wall lit up, and I blinked when one of the panels shifted to reveal a doorway.

Our way out.

I didn't care where the door led, as long as I could make a run for it with Kenan by my side.

That's all that matters.

The distinct voices of two women echoed inside the room, and this time I understood what they were saying.

"We call on you, the Mighty President Foras, to hear our call and take our offering."

The beastly giant inside the summoning chamber was definitely Foras. Whether he was my master or father didn't matter.

He's the leader of my legion.

"The loudest have succeeded," the minion said with a cackle. "The desperate always stand out."

"We call on you, the Mighty President Foras, to hear our call and take our offering."

The voices were very familiar but a soft touch on my wrist scared the shit out of me and I bit down on my tongue before I could cry out.

Kenan's eyes were open and he was staring right at me. When he spotted the huge demon standing over us, his eyes widened with horror.

I held a finger to my lips.

"Our sacrifice is ready to open the pathway completely." Foras whipped a hand in a downward motion and sliced a gash across Kenan's forearm.

Blood glistened from the cut and spilled down the side of the rocky outcrop, dripping down the line etched into the floor and racing to the doorway.

The foggy membrane evaporated and an opening into an alley appeared.

A human alley.

I took a step because I couldn't believe my eyes. I recognized that spot. It was where I'd woken up naked and alone, without a single memory of how I got there. Lost and confused had quickly turned into hungry and scared, before I'd dared to wander out into an unfamiliar world and found somewhere to belong.

"Go to the pathway," Foras instructed.

"Yes, sir."

When the president tried to slice Kenan's other arm, he shifted out of the way at the last minute and tumbled over the other side with a meaty thump.

I helped Kenan to his feet and whispered, "Don't let go of my hand."

He didn't hesitate. "Isn't that the last thing you said to me?"

The feel of his warm palm against mine set off a lovely flow of energy between us.

"Where did he go?" Foras yelled.

The minion glanced over his shoulder. "Where did who go?"

"We call on you, the Mighty President Foras, to hear our call and take our offering."

Foras growled and the room shook. "The blood sacrifice is gone."

"It's of no consequence," the minion said. "Take their essence anyway."

"We call on you, the Mighty President Foras, to hear our call and take our offering."

Foras huffed and puffed like a beefy giant intent on tearing down the house, as he stepped up behind his minion.

"Are you ready?" he asked in his gruff voice.

"It's a pleasure to be of service."

"The pleasure is all mine," Foras said with a laugh.

"We call on you, the Mighty President Foras, to hear our call and take our offering."

"What is it that you want from me?" The minion was the one who addressed the women on the other side.

"We want a treasure that is very dear to us returned," they said in unison.

Why did those voices sound so damn familiar?

My mind reeled as Kenan and I stood close to the two distracted monstrosities, holding hands.

This is how he does it. The Great President of Bullshit answered the desperate pleas of the stupid or desperate, and then sent a willing sucker to the other side.

A surge of anger rushed through me and the sigils responded to my rage.

Kenan shielded his eyes.

"I hope these two are tasty," the minion whispered.

"Humans usually are." Foras pressed a large hand against the back of the minion's head, almost cupping it. "When you get to the other side, you won't remember who you are or where you're from. Your skull will be as empty as a barren field. And if you survive, all of your hellish assets will be lost with time, so cherish every ability while you can."

"Yes, sir."

My blood boiled. I'd probably stood in the same position as the stupid minion. Eager to sacrifice myself on behalf of that asshole, because he wanted to feast on the flesh and souls of unsuspecting humans who didn't suspect what they were getting themselves into.

Foras used his legion as pawns for his own entertainment and gain.

"We call on you, the Mighty President Foras, to hear our call and take our offering."

"Kenan, we need to go through that doorway," I whispered. If we didn't make a break for it soon, we'd lose our only chance to escape. I wasn't about to jeopardize Kenan's life, and I certainly wasn't prepared to lose everything after all the shit we'd gone through.

We're getting out of here right the fuck now.

"How?" he asked.

"Can you run?"

"Yeah." Kenan was pale and blood poured from his forearm but if we didn't leave, they'd spot the drops on the floor. We might be invisible but his blood wasn't.

"We call on you, the Mighty President Foras, to hear our call and take our offering and in return we want you to find a treasure that is very dear to us."

"Yes, what is this treasure you seek?" the minion asked.

"Are you ready?" I said to Kenan.

"Yes."

"Our dear daughter and friend," the women said together. "We summon Destiny back to our side. Where she belongs."

Kenan and I ran under the president's muscled legs.

Foras bent forward as we passed beneath him, and I got a proper glimpse of the women who'd dared to mention an actual name that wasn't his. We cleared the area before he could squash us and Kenan shoved the minion out of the way. The idiot fell sideways, landing like a confused cockroach.

We pushed on, leaped into the doorway a second before my name filled the silence.

Destiny.

I ignored the call because the only thing that mattered was escaping the summoning chamber.

The jump happened in slow motion. With our hands interlaced and legs stretched out in midair, the atmosphere changed instantly. From obsidian with glowing symbols to a darkened alleyway.

"You have only one quest to fulfil by entering the Hellmouth. Go to the summoning chamber, rescue what's yours and don't try to find out anything else. Don't wonder about your origins or get anyone's attention. And don't look back when you leave."

We both landed on our feet inside the alley, short of breath but still alive. The pentagram inscribed on the brick wall in front of us had been made from blood that had turned to rust. When I ran my fingertips over the inscription, it vanished.

The door was sealed.

"We made it!" I threw my arms around Kenan. "We actually fucking made it!"

"Yeah, we did." He collapsed into my arms.

"It worked!" a familiar voice said behind us.

I turned to find Zenda and Mer holding hands in front of the opposite wall. Both seemed relieved and had identical grins.

"What the hell are you two doing here?" I said while untangling myself from Kenan. "That was *you*? But how did you know?"

I couldn't believe it. It was *them* all along. Two strong and powerful women who never gave up. Did Erela orchestrate the summoning? Did she plan for Zenda and Mer to drag us out of Hell?

Zenda rushed over and hugged me tightly. She ran a hand over my hair and loosened the feather but I caught it.

"Thank Goddess you're all right. And you." She reached out to take Kenan's hand and dragged him into the hug. "I thought I'd lost you both."

"But how did you find us?" Tears blurred my vision. They'd gotten me—*us*—out.

"Call it divine intervention," Mer said with a small smile.

The angel had organized our rescue.

"Erela told you." The celestial worked in weird and wonderful ways and I could feel her feather humming in my hand.

Mer shrugged. "It seems you have powerful friends in high places. You've forged strong ties with an angel who risked everything to tell us where to go, what to do and when to do it."

I untangled myself from Zenda and Kenan and went to my friend to embrace her too.

"Thank you." I hadn't known what would happen inside the temple—because that was clearly what it was—or how we got out alive, but ... *Wait a minute.* I pulled out of the embrace and sighed. "I remember."

Everything that happened when I was part of Foras's legion suddenly spilled into my mind. Not only what we'd experienced after Erela pushed me into the Hellmouth but everything before that. The existence I hadn't been able to connect to no matter how hard I'd tried ...

"But I don't want to go." I was smaller in stature, age and personality. Didn't want to be inside the summoning chamber.

"It's an experience we must all go through," Foras—my overbearing father—said, nudging me closer to the open doorway facing a brick wall and a strange man. "You'll be back soon. I promise."

"Are you sure?" I didn't want him to think I was weak. I bit down on my lip hard enough to draw blood.

"Of course." He pressed a hand to the top of my head and threaded something around my horns before sending a wave of fire through my mind.

Until every thought faded and I didn't remember who I was or what I was doing there. The only thing I knew was that I had to step through the wall.

Father pushed me with one hand and grabbed a tight hold of the summoner with the other.

As the human and I traded places, our eyes met.

The memory shattered, but I finally understood the truth.

I recognized the summoner because I'd seen him in many photos. In Zenda's house. The man who'd summoned me, the one Foras devoured, was her partner.

Walter.

She'd told me stories about his bravery and undying thirst for knowledge, how it ultimately led to Walter's demise because he'd betrayed the one who'd loved him the most, and he forfeited his life for the mistake. I'd never made the connection.

Until now.

He'd died because of me. Yet Zenda never held it against me, chose to adopt and nurture me instead. It said a lot about her character and strength. She was one of the bravest and brightest souls I'd ever met.

"Walter," the name slid from my lips.

"I'm very sorry." Zenda took my hand and squeezed. "It was his fault …"

"Is that why I ended up in your yard?"

"Quite possibly."

"Foras made me forget. He lied to me." I waited for the pain of betrayal and hurt to strike, but I didn't care. Foras swapped me for his temporary gain and had no qualms about it. At least I'd bested him by escaping. He might have sent me away, but he'd helped me find a real home with people who loved me.

The two women I trusted the most in this world remained quiet.

"I need to lie down," Kenan said, breaking the silence.

"You certainly do." Zenda checked him over. "You look like you're about to pass out."

"His arm was cut. We have to make sure he …" But when I turned his forearm over, there was nothing there. "It's gone."

"The only thing he brought back was the fatigue of traveling through a hellish portal," his aunt said.

"You guys go home." Mer stepped in front of the wall. "I'll seal this area permanently to make sure no one ever opens a pathway again."

"I'll do it." I placed my fingertips over the bricks, and called on my fire to rise to the surface. But nothing came. "I must be really tired." I reached into the well of fury that usually sloshed inside my stomach but couldn't access it either. "That's strange, my flames are gone."

"And so are your horns," Mer said.

Zenda frowned as she examined me.

"Well, they should be there. It's been a while since I took my glamour meds." I raised a hand to the top of my head and my horns were gone. Even with a glamour, I could feel their aura because they never disappeared completely, just faded from the human eye. "They're really gone!"

Mer shook her head, as if amazed. "In all the excitement, I didn't notice until now."

"You're also … completely naked." Kenan's breathing wasn't back to normal and he had dark circles under his eyes, but he kept checking me out. "And back to how you looked … before …"

"Shit, I am too." He was right, all of the harsh scarlet skin, black nails and even my tail were gone. *I left everything that made me part of his legion behind, forever.*

He slipped his hand in mine and said, "I don't mind that you're naked."

"Kenan!" Zenda scorned.

Mer chuckled as she shook off her coat and handed it to me. "Take this, it'll be enough to keep you covered until you get home."

"Thanks." I dropped Kenan's hand and slipped on her coat, grateful because I could suddenly feel the cold in a way I hadn't before. I tucked the feather into a pocket.

"Do you finally feel like you're where you belong?" Zenda's eyes were expectant, as if she'd speculated about my ongoing inner struggle.

"You have only one quest to fulfil by entering the Hellmouth. Go to the summoning chamber, rescue what's yours and don't try to find out anything else. Don't wonder about your origins or get anyone's attention. And don't look back when you leave."

Erela's words tumbled into my mind, but they weren't instructions, just tasks I'd crossed off my to-do list.

I nodded. "There's no place like home, and this is mine."

A beaming smile lit up Zenda's face.

"Let's get out of here," Kenan said, lacing his fingers through mine.

When he led me out of the alleyway, I turned my back on the past I'd tried hard to remember and now wanted to forget.

It's true what they say, some things are *best left forgotten.*

EPILOGUE

"Are you going to spend all day in front of the mirror?" Kenan sidled up behind me and wrapped his muscled arms around the front of my stomach. He nuzzled my shoulder and I shivered with delight.

I met his gaze in the mirror and smiled. "I'm just getting used to it, that's all."

"There's nothing to get used to. You were sexy as hell with horns, hooves and tail. Now, you're sexy as fuck without them." He squeezed me tighter and skimmed the side of my neck with his warm lips. "Either way, I can't keep my hands off you."

"Well, you'll have to if we're going to get any work done." I leaned my head back against his shoulder. I caught sight of my smooth legs and the heels on my *feet*. No more cloven hooves and fur.

I'd always envied Zenda's style and could finally pull it off. I wore a cute wrap dress with matching black heels, and the outfit suited my curves and long legs.

I'm a real woman.

"Are you sure you don't mind me tagging along?" Kenan teased.

"Well, considering you proved yourself during the most dangerous case we've ever investigated, I think it's fair to say that a meeting with a priest, followed by a simple antique furniture investigation will be easy."

"You never know," he said, swaying our bodies in a slow dance. "There are a lot of cursed and haunted antique pieces in the world, and the odds of Sagar Investigations finding one of them is pretty high."

"You're not wrong there." I pecked his cheek. "Anyway, we better get going. Let me grab my bag and I'll meet you downstairs."

"Sure thing." Kenan spun me around until we were facing each other and pressed his mouth against mine. "Or we could sneak in a quickie before we go."

"What? There's no—"

"There's always time." His mouth was back on mine, and in spite of my words I got caught up in the moment I considered his offer.

"Maybe we could …"

He tucked his fingers under the hem of my dress when the doorbell echoed through the house.

"Shit," he swore, shuffling away. "Saved by the bell."

I laughed. "We'll catch up later." I kissed him lightly. "Can you get that? I'll be right there."

"Sure, but don't stare for too long." He winked at me before leaving the room.

I couldn't help but smile as I watched him leave. Temporarily losing Kenan had made me realize how much he mattered to me. It helped me get over my paranoia about leaving him out of field work. He still planned to follow his academic pursuits but participated in the family investigation business on the side.

A few days after our fateful stopover in Hell, I'd completely lost my demonic physical attributes and powers. The pentagram void tied to my anger was gone and I didn't miss it one bit. The only extraordinary ability that hung around was my uncanny knack for finding lost things via mind-soar.

If I enclosed myself inside the pentagram in my mind-haven with candles burning at each point and escaped spiritually, I could still locate people and objects. As Zenda said: *astral projection at its simplest and divination at its most complex.*

The recovery was still rough, but Kenan helped me pick up the pieces in the most carnal way possible. He spent a lot of time at my place, and without any secrets between us, I'd decided to ask him to move in with me. I wasn't sure if he'd say yes, considering we worked together, but I craved his company more than ever.

"Des!" his voice boomed from downstairs.

I snuck one last peek at my totally human body, smiled at my reflection and grabbed my bag before sneaking a quick peek inside my mind-haven room. I'd placed Erela the Cherubim's feather inside a *Beauty-and-the-Beast*-style glass canister, where it could be safe under several protection spells Zenda and Mer designed specifically.

Maybe I'd need to use the wondrous token someday, maybe I wouldn't, but it was there.

"Des, come on!"

I closed the door and loved the clicking my heels made on the wooden stairs. No more hoof-thumps from me.

"Okay, okay. I'm coming."

"There you are!" He stood in the entryway with Mer and Tera. "Look who's popped in for a visit."

"We're only stopping by to drop something off," Mer said with a grin. "How are you, Destiny?"

"I'm great."

Tera whistled as I approached. "Wow, you look great!"

"I told you she did," her wife said with a nudge. "Anyway, the reason we're here is because Tera wants to give you a present."

"Yeah, I finally finished the portrait I told you about." Tera stepped outside and returned with a canvas almost as tall as she was. "Here it is." When she turned it over to show what she'd created, I caught my breath. "What do you think?"

I took the painting but couldn't take my eyes off the canvas because she'd captured the chamber perfectly. "When did you start working on this?"

Tera shrugged. "A few months ago. Why?"

"No reason, it's lovely." I wanted to say a lot more but none would make much sense to her and might complicate her life further. "Thank you."

"You're welcome." She narrowed her eyes at me. "You really like it?"

"Tera, I love it! This brilliant piece is going to look awesome in my mind-haven. Don't you think, Kenan?"

"Yeah, it's beautiful." He seemed as drawn to the artwork as me.

Tera grinned. She knew the importance of my mind-haven room.

I met her wife's eye and realized Mer already knew about Tera's foresight. I wanted to ask if that was a result of lycanthropy but decided to keep it to myself.

Sometimes it's best to bite your tongue.

"Anyway, sorry for stopping by unannounced," Mer said. "Tera insisted we drop this off right away."

"It's okay. You're always welcome." I reached out and gave Tera a quick hug. "I really, *really* love this but you have to set a price—"

"Nope. It's your next birthday and Christmas present rolled into one." She stepped out of the embrace and waved awkwardly. "Well, see ya!"

Mer nodded and, together, the couple left the house and headed for their car. I was grateful for their friendship.

"This is an amazing work of art, but how did she visualize that place?" Kenan asked, studying the painting.

"I suspect she's got a gift." I checked my phone. "We better get going …"

"Where do you want me to put it for now?"

"Leave it here and we'll hang it up later." As he propped the canvas against the wall, I tried to ignore the orange sigils on the stone temple walls, but couldn't take me eyes off the single white feather floating down past my arms. Or the fact Tera had painted me as the full demoniac I'd become in the town of Hell and inside the domain of Foras the Mighty President.

Tera had captured the moment perfectly. She'd even added the altar behind me and the prone shadow lying on top.

"We really have to go," Kenan said.

"Yeah."

"It feels like everything is coming full circle." He took my hand and I felt the weight of his words. "Especially since we're going to speak to a diocese about finding the missing Sister Trinity."

At least we could handle that. "She's gone but they don't know that. We'll take the case and make up a story about her disappearance." A more dignified fabrication than the truth. "I might even throw in the bombshell about her having a daughter. It should be the easiest money we ever make."

"Wouldn't count on it, the Church has a way of complicating things."

"After going to Hell and back *twice*, helping an angel, outsmarting several demons, and banishing more soulless kids than I care to count … I have nothing to fear from a bunch of holier than thou men in dresses."

"Well, when you put it that way."

"Besides, the nun might've paid us in full but, if they want to keep their dirt under the rug, we're going to be well compensated twice." I had no qualms about ripping off the Church, not after what they did to Sister Trinity. The nun might have given into her fiendish ways, but she'd been put in that situation because they refused to help her save her daughter from possession.

My feelings about Trinity would always be problematic. Sometimes I hated her, and then I felt sorry for the poor nun. But mostly, I remembered how she helped a busload of spirits crossover and guided the trapped children to Erela.

"We should feel bad about some of that, but—"

"We have nothing to feel bad about," I said, cutting him off. "I'm just glad we're both back where we belong and have many future adventures to look forward to."

Kenan's lovely smile made my heart stutter.

"Let's go." I locked the door and we walked to Lady Bug, who was safely parked in the driveway after her overstay outside a shitty motel.

During the last week, I'd faced a lot of important truths and found out the hard way that I shouldn't fear love. And that the friends I found along the way were my real family.

Home really is *where the heart is.*

Acknowledgements

By the time I started writing the first draft of Destiny's story, she'd already been renting space in my head for a while. The idea came to me when I first saw a lovely piece of artwork online, featuring a demonic lady that screamed abandonment issues.

That was several years ago, and since the initial idea, it's gone through several changes.

Firstly, I'd like to thank all the fictional supernatural/paranormal detectives who inspired me to create my own.

Thank you to Brigids Gate Press for publishing Destiny's adventure and giving my story a nice home. I also want to thank Somer Canon and Stephanie Ellis for their attention to detail and for helping me strengthen the story.

My husband deserves a huge thank you and kudos for riding this turbulent publishing wave with me. He's been there since the beginning and has provided endless support. He helps fuel my creative spark.

I need to mention someone else. My beloved familiar, Loki. He passed away a few years ago but he was with me during the writing and revising of *Fallen Destiny*. I miss him a lot and feel like his spirit is embedded in every story I wrote while he kept me company.

And lastly, I want to thank YOU for taking the time to read my book. I hope you enjoyed it!

About the Author

Yolanda Sfetsos lives in Sydney, Australia, with her awesome husband, and writes horror tales that bleed into other genres.

When she's not daydreaming about her dark ideas, she's taking notes on her phone, or sitting at her desk with her laptop. She loves going for long walks that often spark her imagination. She's a bibliophile, and enjoys playing cozy games on her Switch Lite.

She has books published by several indie publishers, has self-published another, and her debut short story collection was released in 2025 by Cemetery Gates Media.

Visit her website: www.yolandasfetsos.com

More From Brigids Gate Press

THE WOLF AND THE FAVOUR

Catherine McCarthy

Ten-year-old Hannah has Down syndrome and oodles of courage, but should she trust the alluring tree creature who smells of Mamma's perfume or the blue-eyed wolf who warns her not to enter the woods under any circumstance?

The Wolf and the Favour is a tale of love, trust, and courage. A tale that champions the neurodivergent voice and proves the true power of a person's strength lies within themselves.

DANGEROUS WATERS

ed. Julia C. Lweis

Malevolent mermaids.

Sinister sirens.

Scary selkies.

And other dangerous women of the deep blue sea.

Dangerous waters takes us deep beneath the ocean waves and shows us once more why we need to be cautious about venturing out into the water.

Featuring stories, drabbles and poems by Sandra Ljubjanović, John Higgins, Patrick Rutigliano, Candace Robinson, Emmanuel Williams, Desirée M. Niccoli, L. Marie Wood, Samantha Lokai, Christina Henneman, Gully Novaro, Christine Lukas, Alice Austin, Dawn Vogel, Victoria Nations, Mark Towse, Kristin Cleaveland, Ben Monroe, Kurt Newton, E.M. Linden, Eva Papasoulioti, Ann Wuehler, Rachel Dib, A.R. Fredericksen, Daniel Pyle, Megan Hart, Ef Deal, Katherine Traylor, Juliegh Howard-Hobson, Simon Kewin, Elana Gomel, Lauren E. Reynolds, Grace R. Reynolds, René Galván, Marshall J. Moore, Ngo Binh Anh Khoa, Roxie Vorhees, April Yates, Kaitlin Tremblay, T.K. Howell, Kayla Whittle, Emily Y. Teng, Briana McGuckin, Tom Farr, Cassandra Taylor, Steven-Elliot Altman, Paul M. Feeney, Lucy Collins, Marianne Halbert, Rosie Arcane, Antonia Rachel Ward, Steven Lord, and Jessica Peter.

DISSONANCE OF BIRD SONG

Alexandra Beaumont

In the storm-riven wilds of ancient Cornwall the sea's whisper will charm us all.

Dissonance of Bird Song is the folkloric-fantasy tale of Eseld, a song-weaver fleeing her home to cure the sacred birds of her people and save her sister. Locked between the lies of land-dwellers and the snare of an ancient sea queen, Eseld must fight to find her own path. Amidst a storm of betrayal and heartbreak, what will Eseld sacrifice to save the ones she loves?

Readers who enjoyed Lucy Hounsom's *Sistersong*, Naomi Novik's *Uprooted*, and Natasha Bowen's *Skin of the Sea* will love *Dissonance of Bird Song*.

BRIGIDS GATE PRESS

THE HIDING

Alethea Lyons

Arcane archivist Harper has always been plagued by dreams of grotesque creatures and bloody deaths. When she bumps into a ghostwalker in the Shambles and has a visceral experience of his execution, she knows it's a foretelling. Yet fear of the Queen's Guard stops her speaking out. When her vision indeed comes true, the unusual markings on the ghostwalker's corpse, combined with his neatly excised vocal cords, send a ripple of terror through York.

The witch hunt is on. As the body count rises, Harper knows her magic is the only way to find the killer – if she can avoid being hanged as a witch. To protect both human and supernatural, Harper walks the thin line between their worlds. She and her demonhunter foster-sister form a multi-faith team with a forensic scientist, a spirit Harper accidentally summoned, and a techno-witch, to catch the killer before more people die.

Visit our website at: www.brigidsgatepress.com